ABOUT THIS BOOK

She might be a girly girl, but she never imagined being an actual unicorn princess—or that her own mother would seek to destroy her.

Thea has no idea what her future holds. When she's whisked off to a mysterious town in the mountains, she finds out magic is real—and so are unicorns.

If that wasn't shocking enough, she also learns that her mom's an evil sorceress who desires to destroy the unicorns, and all of Havenwood Falls is in danger. Thea has until her eighteenth birthday to learn how to control her magic, lead the herd, and maybe kiss the cute girl at Havenwood Stables.

HAVENWOOD FALLS HIGH BOOKS

Predestined by Valia Lind

Rediscovered by Morgan Wylie

Ashes of Fate by Apryl Baker

Stay up to date at www.HavenwoodFalls.com

BOOKS BY MEGAN LINSKI

The Fire Prophecy (Academy of Magical Creatures Book #1) – Co-written with Alicia Rades

The Water Legacy (Academy of Magical Creatures Book #2) – Co-written with Alicia Rades

The Earth Legend (Academy of Magical Creatures Book #3) – Co-written with Alicia Rades

The Air Omen (Academy of Magical Creatures Book #4) – Co-written with Alicia Rades

The Wolven Mark (University of Sorcery Book #1)

Kingdom From Ashes (The Kingdom Saga Book #1)

Fallen From Ashes (The Kingdom Saga Book #2)

Redemption From Ashes (The Kingdom Saga Book #3)

Prince of Fire (The Kingdom Saga Book #4)

Dawn From Embers (The Kingdom Saga Book #5)

Blessings From Ashes (A Kingdom Saga Novella)

Court of Vampires (The Shifter Prophecy Book #1)

Den of Wolves (The Shifter Prophecy Book #2)

War of Witches (The Shifter Prophecy Book #3)

Heir to Russia (The Shifter Prophecy Book #4)

Torrent (Angels & Demons Book #1)

Torture (Angels & Demons Book #2)

Truth (Angels & Demons Book #3)

Song of Smoke and Fire (Song of Dragonfire Book #1)

Change of Wind and Storms (Song of Dragonfire Book #2)

World of Gods and Men (Song of Dragonfire Book #3)

Rhodi's Light (The Rhodi Saga Book #1)

Rhodi Rising (The Rhodi Saga Book #2)

Rhodi's Lullaby (The Rhodi Saga Book #3)

Kiatana's Journey (Creatures of the Lands Book #1) – Co-written with Krisen Lison

Vera's Song (Creatures of the Lands Book #2) – Co-written with Krisen Lison

Wyntier's Rise (Creatures of the Lands Book #3) – Co-written with Krisen Lison

Vixen's Fate (Creatures of the Lands Book #4) – Co-written with Krisen Lison

Midnightstar (Creatures of the Lands Book #5) – Co-written with Krisen Lison

Angel's Rebellion (Creatures of the Lands Book #6) – Co-written with Krisen Lison

Breathless (Twisted Fairy Tales Shared Series Book #1)

Alora (Standalone)

These Starcrossed Lives of Ours (Standalone)

Sign of the Griffin (Standalone)

Eerie Tales (A Short Story Collection)

Webs & Roses (A Poetry Collection)

Anything But (Razberry Sweet Book #1)

Save Me (Razberry Sweet Book #2)

The Witch's Curse (Free Short Story)

UNICORN'S LAMENT

A HAVENWOOD FALLS HIGH NOVELLA

MEGAN LINSKI

This novel is dedicated to all the unicorns out there—the people who society thinks are different, but really, they just shine brighter than all the others.

CHAPTER 1

*T*he same dream haunted me every night.

I followed the silver unicorn through the gray, misty forest. I never got quite close enough to see many details, but I knew he was a stallion—he had huge muscles and stood at a height that would tower over me, if I dared to get near. His coat was shinier than the edge of a sharpened knife, and his rippling mane and tail went past his knees.

But the most incredible thing about him was the golden horn that stuck out of the middle of his forehead. It shimmered and sparkled, even in the cloudy day, and seemed to gleam when he looked toward me.

I chased the stallion through the woods. But though I ran as fast as I could, winding through trees and ducking branches, the unicorn was always faster. Just as I was about to reach out and pet his coat, he raced off into the trees and vanished.

Then I woke up.

I started upright in bed. My chest heaved as if I'd been running. I took a few deep breaths and tried to steady myself.

Just another dream, Thea. It's not real.

I hated that it wasn't real. Something about that unicorn made me feel empty inside without him.

But unicorns weren't real, and neither were dreams. Shaking off how vivid it felt, I stumbled out of bed and forced myself to take a cold shower, allowing the water to roll down my back, trying to wake myself up.

I couldn't. Even though I tried, the dream followed me around all day.

Havenwood Village was a nice apartment complex—certainly the best I'd ever lived in. I liked that I had my own bathroom. My mom had landed a good job at the Havenwood Falls Medical Center, and for the first time in a long while, we were doing fine.

First time since the fire, I guess.

I threw my white-blond hair up into a ponytail, slipping on a pair of jeans and a racerback top. I longed to grab the pink dress and sparkly heels in the corner of my closet and change into that instead, but I reminded myself that wasn't who I was anymore.

Ambrosia was already at the stove in the kitchen, making pancakes.

"How did you sleep, honey?" she asked as I sat at the table, placing a stack of pancakes in front of me. They were topped with raspberries, whipped cream, and sprinkles, just how I liked them.

"Fine, Ambrosia," I lied. My mother never wanted me to call her Mom, just always by her first name. It'd been like that since I was a little girl. It was a little weird to some people, but I was used to it.

She noticed the bags under my eyes and said, "You should be sleeping in. School will start pretty soon, and you won't be able to."

"I know." It was early August. My eighteenth birthday was thirty days away, at the end of the month. I'd be starting my senior year at Havenwood Falls High soon.

I hated starting a new school this close to graduation, but at the same time, Havenwood Falls High couldn't possibly be worse than Desmona Prep back in the Big Easy. That place had been hell on earth.

"Why don't you go to the lake later? There are plenty of people your age swimming, I'd bet. It's going to be such a nice day," Ambrosia suggested.

"I'm not one much for friends." I liked to keep to myself. I shoveled my pancakes into my mouth and enjoyed every bite of them. Yep. Solitude and food. Peace, quiet, and sweets were all a girl needed.

"You know," Ambrosia started, and she sat down on the other side of the table to eat her own pancakes, "I heard there's a riding stable nearby."

That piqued my interest. "Really?"

"Yep. Trains jumpers." She reached around to the drawers behind her, pulled open one of them, and handed me a brochure. I read it quickly.

Havenwood Stables. Looked like a fancy place, the kind where Olympians would train. I hadn't ridden a horse since I'd left Desmona Prep. I was dying to get back on one again. "How much do they charge?"

"What if I told you I already paid for a full semester's worth of lessons?" Ambrosia held her mug of coffee and smiled.

"No freaking way!" I shouted. "Ambrosia, you're the best!"

I got up and hugged her. It only took a few minutes for me to rush back into my room, change into a pair of breeches and knee-high boots, and grab my riding helmet.

"It's close enough you can walk," Ambrosia said. She got out a map of the town, took a red marker, and drew a path before she handed it to me.

I grabbed it and headed for the door. I was practically running to get there.

"Stick to the main road," Ambrosia warned me. She sounded serious about it. "Don't go into the woods. I mean it."

"Yes, Ambrosia." I hurried outside. It was still early morning, and a bit chilly out. I should've grabbed a jacket. I shivered, hoping the temperature would get back up to the forecasted seventy-five quick. The climate was way different here than it was in Louisiana. I was used to frying out there. Here I'd have to deal with snow, something I'd hardly seen before. I was a bit nauseated from the high altitude, though it was beginning to subside now that I was up and moving.

As I walked, I took in the sights of my new home. It was small, but Havenwood Falls was a nice place. Idyllic. Charming, even. But it was more than a little weird. The vibe that came off of it was . . . odd. It was nothing like New Orleans, which I missed, but not enough to want to go back.

I thought it wasn't a quiet town, either. I'd only been living here a few days, but just from walking around the area, I got the sense that every resident here had some kind of secret to hide.

I looked at the map Ambrosia had drawn. The stables were to the west, just outside of town. I could stick to the main road, as she said, and get there most likely in a half hour or so.

But it looked like there was a shortcut I could take—near the woods by the Mathews River. It seemed like rough terrain, but I bet it'd cut my walk time in half.

I was never very good at following the rules, so I left the sidewalk and veered into the trees, crossing over a creek by way of a small homemade bridge someone had built. I had a good sense of direction and could tell which way was west, so I kept walking that way, figuring I'd hit the horse stables sooner or later.

It didn't take me long to realize that I was lost. But I didn't mind it. I liked wandering. There's something nice about feeling like you are the only person in the world. I enjoyed my walk through the greenery, taking in the smells of fresh morning dew on the pine trees and listening to the birds chirping.

Then I heard something—the crack of a branch.

I whirled around. My eyes went wide when I saw what was standing above me.

On an embankment overhead stood a horse—but it wasn't a horse at all. It was the unicorn. Even more, it was *my* unicorn, and he was real. He stood proudly, his head held high and his ears pointing toward me. His silver coat shone in a halo of light the sun had formed around him, and his golden horn glistened, just like it did in my dream. His nostrils flared as he observed me, taking me in.

I took a step forward. But as soon as I moved, the unicorn took off and disappeared into the trees.

I stood there frozen for a few seconds, struggling to comprehend what had just happened. Yeah. Havenwood Falls was definitely different.

CHAPTER 2

I came out of the woods and ended up staring at a large commercial barn surrounded by paddocks. I could smell horses from here. The pastures were filled with all kinds of horses, of all breeds.

The barn was red in color and probably the biggest I'd ever seen. It was surprising that such a small town had such a huge training arena. I walked up the gravel road and looked to my right.

There was already a rider in the outdoor training arena, warming up. She rode a large Thoroughbred gelding and was sailing over jumps that had been set up in a pattern around the arena.

She was the most beautiful girl I'd ever seen. I had to stop in my tracks and watch her for a minute as she and her horse flew effortlessly over the jumps. Her hair was long and blond, darker than mine, and was in a ponytail under her helmet. Her skin was pale—looked fragile, even—and roses dotted her cheeks.

Her eyes . . . Something about her eyes was different. They were large and blue, and sparkled every time her horse took a leap of faith.

After she was done with the course, she stopped her horse for a moment and smiled at me. The expression made my stomach do flip-flops.

I was lame, so I more or less stood there frozen until the rider moved her horse on. I forced myself to head inside the barn, berating myself for how stupid I probably looked. Why couldn't I have waved or something? I probably looked like some zombie or freak.

My face was bright red. I could feel it. I headed into the barn and looked for someone who was probably in charge.

There were two people inside. One was a girl around my age. She had light brown hair and was mucking a stall. The other was a tall dude, middle-aged, with dark skin, short-cropped hair, and a look that instantly told me he was a hardass. He was muscular enough that he looked like he could lift a car no sweat.

I glanced again at the brunette. Her eyes shone just like the girl outside when she spotted me. Weird.

"Hi," I said. "My mother signed me up for riding lessons here. I'm looking for the person to talk to?"

The man turned my way. His expression seemed cold, distant. He barely moved as he raised an eyebrow and said, "And you are?"

"Uh . . ." What a rude way to start a conversation with someone. "The name on the list should be Aramanthe Amorea. Thea for short," I said.

His face changed when I said my name, but only slightly. A semblance of shock crossed over it before it quickly righted itself again, and he said, "We've been waiting for you. I'm the head instructor here at Havenwood Stables. You may call me Avalar."

"Oh." This guy had such a formal way of speaking. It was awkward. "Okay. So when should I come back for my first lesson?"

"You may start today," Avalar replied. "A group lesson will begin in about fifteen minutes. You're required to attend at least three before you move on to private lessons—to make sure you're serious."

He turned and waved his hand behind him as an indication for me to follow. I certainly wouldn't get a warm welcome from him. He stopped next to the stall where the girl was.

"This is Ransom," Avalar said, gesturing to a gray Arabian gelding. "He'll be your mount for the time you are here."

"I prefer mares, actually," I said.

"Well, this should be a good challenge for you, then." Avalar said. His tone was harsh and rude.

I decided I hated the guy. Avalar was definitely a jerk. *He* was gonna be my jumping coach? Swell.

Avalar looked to the girl next to me. "Novah, can you help Thea tack up?"

"Sure thing!" Novah said brightly. Her smile was huge. She was the complete opposite of Avalar.

"Class will begin on time. Hurry along to make sure you're not left behind." That was all the goodbye he gave me before Avalar stalked off. I was left standing behind, wondering if it had been a good decision for Ambrosia to prepay for all of my lessons here.

"Don't worry about Avalar," Novah said, noticing my stricken expression. "He's a pain to get along with, but he'll lighten up once he gets used to you."

"I hope so," I mumbled under my breath. Something about the guy was just . . . off.

"Come on. I'll show you around." Novah led me to the tack room, where she helped me saddle up and put a bridle on Ransom. He was strong and high-spirited, which became apparent when I tried to put the bit in his mouth. He was going to be fun to ride, I bet.

"You been riding long?" Novah asked brightly. She led her horse out into the hallway, a fat quarter horse mare, to wait for me.

"Practically all my life," I responded. Ransom tried to headbutt me, and I had to push him away.

"Me too," Novah said. "Sera and I are both like that. It's so nice to meet new friends with the same interests as you."

Sera . . . "Was she the one practicing on the Thoroughbred earlier?"

"Yep." Novah said it like she was proud. "She's amazing, isn't she? I love watching her ride. She has a way with horses, but—" Novah giggled. "I think you and I can both say that we do, too."

This girl didn't even know me, but she acted like we were already best friends for life. Novah talked all the way out to the paddock, where Avalar was already instructing Sera. I didn't say much. I'd learned at Desmona Prep to keep my head down and stay in my lane.

Not that Novah needed any responses from me. She was the kind of girl who loved to talk.

When we got to the mounting block, I swung myself up onto Ransom and joined the lesson, taking a few warm-up trots and canters around the arena, watching Sera perform her jumps. Avalar noticed me immediately.

"Thea," he said. "I'd like to see what you can do. Take the course and try to copy Sera."

I took a look at the poles. They were set at a height that I'd jumped before, but never on a new horse and never after such a long span between rides. I'd hardly been on a horse all summer due to the move. It was clear that Avalar wasn't letting me off easy.

But I wasn't one to back down from a challenge. "Sure."

I urged Ransom into a canter, and set my sights on the first jump. Novah fell to the side, chatting with Sera, while Sera herself watched me with interest. I definitely felt the pressure.

I pictured myself sailing over the first jump. I steadied myself, and Ransom eagerly took it. I felt a thrill go through my body, entering through my stomach, as we crossed over it with ease. We took the next jump just as easily, and the next, too. My brain went numb with the thrill of it as we neared the end of the course. I was going to do a perfect practice round, on my first time!

Then my eyes glanced over to Sera, and I noticed her whispering to Novah. Was she saying something about me? I lost concentration, and the next jump came up too quick.

I misdirected Ransom. True to the Arabian he was, he slid to a stop before the jump and bucked, sending me flying off. I went hurtling through the air and crashed into the poles, destroying the jump completely.

"Thea!" I heard Novah call. "Are you okay?"

My head was spinning, but all my limbs were intact. Slowly, I got to my feet. "Yeah. Yeah, I'm okay."

Avalar expressed no sense of concern. "A fair attempt," he said. "Though clearly nothing special."

What was it with this guy? It's like he had something personal against me. I dusted off the dirt, grabbed Ransom's reins, and got back up on him, to show Avalar that I wasn't done.

Avalar was already reconstructing the jump. "Novah. You're up next."

Novah moved forward. I walked Ransom to the side of the arena with my head held down, not daring to look up at Sera. Great. I'd totally fallen on my ass in front of a really cute girl. She probably thought I was some amateur who'd never ridden a horse in my life.

A few minutes passed, and I smelled the scent of some sort of flowery perfume—an expensive one, like Versace or Coach. I didn't know anyone who wore perfume to the barn. I heard hoofbeats beside me, and looked up to see Sera beside me on her Thoroughbred.

"You shouldn't be embarrassed. I've fallen hundreds of times on these jumps," she said. "It's the first time I've seen a newcomer finish them so well."

Even her voice sounded beautiful—like musical wind chimes, or some celebrity singing your favorite song. My mouth went dry, and my mind went blank. *Say something!* my mind screamed, but I was too shy.

She seemed to notice that I wasn't going to say anything, and said, "I'm Sera. I've been here for a while. Did you just move to Havenwood Falls?"

I woke up then, and said, "Yeah, a few days ago. I'm still trying to get the hang of things around here."

"Novah and I will show you around later. This place is amazing. You'll see why." She winked at me, and butterflies danced inside my stomach.

We didn't get much time to talk after that, because Avalar started pushing us hard during the practice. We did lots of drills, and so many exercises that my muscles started to ache and I was sweating pretty badly. It no longer felt cool out. But I liked it. I could feel my skills getting better and better the longer the practice went on.

As much as I couldn't stand him, Avalar knew a lot about jumping and horses. He'd make sure I stayed focused and disciplined. He was the kind of coach that I needed to have if I wanted to make the Olympics someday.

Which sucked, because our personalities totally clashed.

"That's enough for today," Avalar said around noon. "We'll pick this up next session. You are dismissed."

I'd never had an instructor end a lesson like a military drill. Avalar ran a tight ship. The three of us walked to cool the horses off, then untacked them in the stables.

I listened to Novah and Sera chat about an album some singer had dropped while I brushed Ransom down. I'd grown to like Ransom during our lesson. He was headstrong, but fun to ride.

"You hungry, Thea?" Sera peeked her head around the stall door. "There's this amazing burger place in town that has the best shakes. It would be a great way to start off your tour of Havenwood Falls."

"Um . . ." I didn't know what to say. I hadn't been asked to hang with anyone in forever.

I decided to take a leap of faith. It wasn't a date, anyhow.

"Sure. I'll come." I gestured to my clothes. "Though I'm not exactly dressed for it." I was covered in dirt and horse slime from the ride.

"We can go to my house. It's not far. I'll lend you some things." Sera flashed me another brilliant smile, and my heart skipped a beat.

There was the sound of boots, and I glanced up. A tall guy with brown hair and freckles was leaning against Novah's stall. He looked like he was a senior in high school, like me. I didn't pay much attention to him while I finished with Ransom. Boys were okay, but I wasn't into them.

Novah, though. She had guy crazy written all over her, and it showed. "Hey, Jas." She twirled a strand of hair around her finger. "How are you doing?"

He leaned against a stall door and gave her a smile that probably made her knees go weak. "Just fine, Novah Bell."

He reached out to tweak her nose, and she giggled.

"I was thinking you girls would like to come out to the lake," Jas said. "Big party going on there tonight."

"Not today, Jas," Sera said. "Today's a girls' day."

Her words seemed to carry a heavier meaning. His face became serious, and Jas said, "Right. Catch you girls later."

Jas walked away, and my eyes followed him as he left. What the heck. Did everything in this town seem to be one big teen movie?

Novah sighed. "That party sounds like fun. I bet Jas looks so hot in his swim trunks. I'm totally gonna miss out on that bod."

"Later, Novah." Sera's words seemed fierce. Then she looked at me, and her tone lightened again. "Come on. Let's get you changed. I'm starving."

Sera took me back to her car—a light blue turquoise truck that was probably older than most grandpas. It was vintage, and totally cool. She drove us a mile or so up the road to a big house up one of the mountains, one with a couple of fancy cars in the driveway.

I texted Ambrosia to tell her where I was, and the response I got from her was thrilled. She was happy I was making new friends already. I didn't have any, not for all the time I went to Desmona Prep.

I was impressed when we walked inside. Sera's house had marble floors and chandeliers, with a staircase that wrapped upward in a spiral. I was wary about meeting parents, but I didn't see any.

Sera's room was bigger than my entire apartment. And it looked like the color turquoise blue had gone wild in here. It was everywhere, from the paint on the walls to the dresser to the fluffy throw pillows. Dozens of stuffed animals, most of them horses, were strewn on the bed and in piles beside girly magazines and makeup.

Sera's room looked like the sort you'd find in a teen movie, or in an interior decorating magazine. I was sort of jealous, before I thought a girl as pretty as her deserved it.

Sera instantly began rifling through her giant closet, which contained more blues. "Now, where is it . . ."

She finally pulled out a pink romper, one that was decorated with flowers, and jeweled sandals. "Here. Put these on."

"No, I—" I hadn't worn something that girly since . . . When was the last time I worn something girly, anyhow? I don't even think I'd worn anything with a flower on it in months.

"Please? You'll look amazing in it," Sera begged, her eyes large and pleading.

I couldn't really say no to her. I grabbed it, but hesitated. It didn't bother me to change in front of Novah, but Sera was a different story.

She seemed to notice my discomfort and turned around, busying herself by going to the bathroom. Novah kept going on and on about Jas while I changed.

"Do you think Jas will like this one, or this one?" Novah slipped on a pair of shorts and yanked off her shirt. She stood in her bra while she held up two different shirts, light green in color, asking for my opinion.

"No idea. I just met him," I said. I'd just met these girls, too, but it didn't look like it mattered. They'd adopted me, apparently.

"I'll go with this one. It makes my boobs look good," Novah said before she slipped it on.

When Sera returned, she was wearing a long blue sundress that amplified her curves. Sera let out a squeal when she saw me. "OMG! It looks amazing on you!"

"Does it?" I didn't know.

"Yes. You have such an amazing body," Sera said. She ran her hands up and down my arms, and I felt goosebumps rise there.

Novah and Sera weren't content to let us leave until they had done my makeup and curled my hair. When they finally nestled a jeweled headband between my curls, one that had a bow, I looked in the mirror and hardly recognized myself. I felt more like myself than I had in ages.

Sera spritzed me with some of her perfume and said, "There. You're perfect."

The compliment made me blush. We piled back in her truck, and Sera and Thea blasted the radio and sang along to country music. They had beautiful voices, I noticed, and harmonized in all the right parts. I sang along quietly under my breath, hoping they didn't realize I was off-key.

I noticed as we drove, Sera's clothes smelled like her, too. I really liked that.

When we got to the restaurant, some place called Burger Bar, amazing smells hit my nose. The three of us curled up together in one of the booths. I was worried about being the weird one, but I was happy when both Sera and Novah ordered veggie burgers and tater tots.

"We're both vegetarians," Novah explained when she saw my confused face. "Meat isn't really our thing. We don't like the taste."

"Me either," I admitted, shocked. Just how much did I have in common with these girls?

When I took the first bite of my veggie burger, I almost died. It was that heavenly. This place was the best. The other girls thought so too, because we didn't do much talking as we chowed down.

Some skater boy had sauntered up to our table. "Hey ladies," he said. "Who's the new girl in town?"

His navy-blue eyes were directly on me. Sera grimaced and said, "Thea, this is Dalton Underwood. Also known as our residential annoyance."

"So are you fitting in at Havenwood Falls?" The words seemed to have a double meaning.

"Dalton," Sera said in what seemed like a warning tone. "She doesn't know."

Didn't know? Didn't know what?

"Really? Seems like you two are hiding secrets." Dalton suppressed a laugh.

"Stick to your own kind, Dalton," Novah snapped.

Dalton grinned and added, "I get the point. I was just gonna get on out of here, anyhow. See you around, Thea."

He gave me a long stare—like he knew something about me that I didn't—before he left Burger Bar. I watched him cruise off on his skateboard from the window.

There was something . . . different about him. I wasn't sure what. I could just sense it. Like vibrations or something.

But that was weird. I pushed Dalton out of my mind and tried to focus back on my food.

"Ignore Dalton," Novah said. "He's an instigator. Likes to . . . tease us."

Like I knew what that meant. Were Sera and Novah hiding something? I wasn't sure. Maybe Dalton was just messing with me.

"You want to share my shake, Thea? I can't finish it," Sera started. She pushed it toward me and put another straw in.

I gulped, until I told myself it wasn't anything. I leaned forward and started drinking from the shake. As I did, Sera took a straw in her mouth and started drinking, too, so that our foreheads were nearly touching.

My mouth was so close to her lips. They looked so soft, wrapped around that straw. As I was drinking, I couldn't help but get sucked into her eyes again. Damn. This was a really good milkshake.

"Thea and Sera alert," Novah said, waving her hand and snapping us both out of it. "What are we doing after this?"

Sera pulled away from the milkshake and said, "I figured we could go to Callie's Consignments and look for new dresses."

"Finally," Novah said, exasperated. "I need a new wardrobe. I don't think the clothes I've been wearing have caught Jas's eye."

"You don't need to look nice to get a boy to like you. Just be yourself," I suggested.

Novah scoffed. "Believe me, honey, I've tried. But Jas doesn't have very much going on up there, and he doesn't even notice me unless I got these puppies out."

She grabbed her boobs. Sera fell on the table laughing, and I allowed myself to join in. These girls were kinda fun.

"That's not true." Sera wiped her eyes and looked at Novah. "Jas likes you, Novah. I know it."

"Well, at any rate, a new dress won't hurt," Novah insisted. She practically sprung up from the booth. "Come on, girls. I need to strengthen the artillery."

At the consignment shop, neither Sera nor Novah tried anything on unless it was blue, green, or so ridiculously feminine that its girliness punched you in the face. I mostly stayed on the sidelines and commented on their outfits as they tried on dress after dress.

Novah tried on some outfits that . . . uh . . . *endorsed* what she had to offer, while Sera remained pretty conservative. But whatever she tried on, I thought she looked great in everything. Even some weird old dress from the seventies that looked like drapery, had shoulder pads, and smelled like mothballs.

We weren't the only people taking up the dressing room. Some girl that looked like freaking Taylor Swift was ordering around her boyfriend as she tried on dress after dress, like she expected him to follow her instructions. I thought I overheard that her name was Celeste, and her boyfriend's name was Jonathan.

"Jonathan, can you please hold these?" Celeste put a ton of clothes into Jonathan's arms. I was surprised he didn't buckle under their weight. Celeste kept on piling on more clothes, until she went to the register and tried to talk the shop owner into giving her a deal. Jonathan didn't say much, just kept quiet and did as Celeste said. It was like he was trying to make himself invisible or something. For a moment, I thought he was, because I didn't see him anywhere, but I figured it was just a trick of the eyes. I felt the same weird vibrations coming off them as I did Dalton earlier.

"Thea, I think you should try this on." Sera had gone through the racks for the millionth time, and pulled out a pink dress, one that was floor length and made of satin, with a keyhole neckline. It had blue peeking out from underneath two swaths of pink fabric, decorative swirls adorning the dress.

It was daring, but I did like the outfit. It looked like a cosplay costume, or maybe a unique outfit someone had worn to prom. "Okay. I'll try it on."

In the changing room, my mind was going a million miles an hour. I really wanted to ask Sera if she liked girls, but I was too afraid.

I didn't want to get my heart broken and get turned down again, so I kept silent. I was probably fooling myself. Sera definitely had a boyfriend, and if she didn't, guys were probably lining up to take her on a date. She'd probably laugh in my face if I asked her out.

I was about ready to come out of the changing room and show the girls what I had on, but I heard whispering voices, one of which spoke my name. I shuffled around in the changing room to make it seem like I was still changing, when in reality, I was listening intently to the conversation going on outside my door.

"Thea just got here. She's not ready," Sera insisted.

"We can't keep it from her forever. We have less than a month before *she* shows up," Novah insisted. "Thea deserves to know the truth."

Sera hesitated before she said, "All right. Tonight it is."

It was hard to breathe. Who exactly was *she*, anyway? Had these girls been instructed to be my friends?

I felt offended. Of course they didn't really like me. Who'd want to be my friend, anyhow?

I stepped out of the changing room. Both girls gasped.

"Oh, Thea," Sera breathed. Her eyes ran up and down me. "It's gorgeous on you."

"You think?" I did a little twirl.

Novah nodded. "Yes. It's incredible."

I looked at the price tag. I didn't have much, but being a consignment dress, it wasn't expensive, plus it was on sale.

"Hey, Thea," Sera asked, and I looked up. "After the party at the lake, some of our friends are going to be camping out overnight. Novah and I are going. Would you like to come with, have a sleepover?"

This was my chance to get some answers about whatever they'd been talking about. "Sure. I'd love to."

"Great." Sera beamed. "Pick you up at eight."

I decided to buy the dress. Sera dropped me off at my apartment, promising to come back and pick me up tonight.

I tried to preoccupy myself until then by reading a book, but it was hard. I had a million questions. The unicorn in the woods. Avalar. Sera and Novah's strange behavior. It didn't add up.

Something weird was going on here. And I was going to find out what it was, tonight.

CHAPTER 3

*W*hen Sera came to pick me up at eight o'clock, Novah was already in the truck. It was obvious she and Sera were attached at the hip. I threw my sleeping bag and a change of clothes into the bed before I got in the cab.

I kept waiting for someone to break the ice by announcing some huge secret, but it never came. Sera and Novah kept talking about normal stuff. I waited anxiously, hoping they'd spill the beans about whatever they were hiding at any moment.

It didn't come before we arrived at the party, where a makeshift campsite had been set up by the lake. Novah and Sera got to setting up our tent, but Jas quickly stepped in.

"Let me help you with that, ladies." Jas got on with setting the tent up, but he wasn't very good at it. He kept falling on top of it and putting the poles in the wrong places. I sighed and took pity on him.

"Here, Jas." I took the stuff from him and had the tent set up within a couple of minutes. "It's seriously not that hard."

"My hero," Sera said, looking at me. I blushed again.

I looked around. It really wasn't a big party. About ten or so people, besides us. I went to grab a wine cooler, and I noticed at the table, all the food was vegetarian. No meat to be found. Strange at a barbecue. Did Sera and Novah bring me to the Havenwood Falls Annual Vegan Picnic or something?

Parties weren't really my thing. It wasn't too long before I was bored. I had nobody to talk to, seeing as how Novah was too busy chatting with Jas to notice me, and Sera had just vanished shortly after we arrived. Where had she run off to?

I decided to try to find her. She wasn't at the party or the surrounding area, so I took a hiking trail around the lake to see if she was anywhere nearby.

No luck. I returned to the campsite feeling frustrated. By this time, it was past ten o'clock and dark. Novah was already inside our tent, putting on this gooey-looking face cream and wrapping her hair in curlers.

"I'd figure you'd be inside Jas's tent, trying to get your freak on," I teased.

"Oh, no." Novah blushed. "Jas hasn't even kissed me yet. Though I wish he would."

"Do you know where Sera is?" I peeked out of the tent one more time, just to be sure she wasn't there.

"No." Novah shook her head. "But she's fine. Trust me, she can take care of herself."

I didn't know what that meant. Was Sera some sort of tae kwon do master or something? Who knew.

I figured she'd come back when she was ready. I changed into my pajamas, then cuddled up into my sleeping bag, hoping that I'd wake up the moment Sera returned.

I woke up in the grass outside. I guessed it had to be past three a.m. by the lack of light in the woods. It felt like I'd slept for hours. I listened for the sounds of the campsite, and blearily looked around, but didn't see or hear any signs of it. I was in the middle of the woods.

I sleepwalked sometimes, but not often. Most of the time, it had been when I was little, and I always ended up in the grass. I was glad some freaking cougar hadn't found me or something. I went to stand up, to try to find the campsite again.

I yawned and walked to the river, to splash myself awake. But when I went to kneel down, I found that I couldn't. I extended my hand, only to see that my hand . . . had become a hoof.

Holy. Crap.

I startled awake when I saw my reflection in the water, for I didn't see a human, but a unicorn.

My coat. It was pink. A light pink, almost white. I had a dished nose and long ears. A sparkling white horn grew out of the center of my forehead, and a wavy mane and tail drifted in the wind behind me. A soft pinkness glowed around me, almost like . . . magic.

This was the craziest dream. But if this was a dream, it was a rad one, and I was going to enjoy every single moment of it.

I let out a whoop, but it came out as a whinny instead. I jumped over the river and galloped forward, extending my long legs.

This was a thrill. A gust of exhilaration flew through my body as I rushed forward, running as fast as I could under the light of the stars and moon. My mane and tail flew behind me, and the trees and grasses became a blur. I broke through the trees and entered into an open valley. I threw my head around happily, feeling more free than I ever had in my life. The feeling that was running through me was so strong and powerful it would've brought tears to my eyes, if I had the ability to cry. I just felt so . . . triumphant and powerful and strong.

I noticed that two unicorn mares came up beside me, one on each side. They were slower than I was and drifted behind me. They wanted to run with me. I nickered a welcome and charged forward.

"Thea, slow down! You're going to go over the border," a familiar voice in my head shouted.

That voice stopped me in my tracks. I skidded to a halt, panting and heaving. I'd been running for a while.

The other unicorns stopped beside me. I had the chance to get a good look at them. The first mare was green and had a horn that curled and spiraled instead of one that was straight. Her mane and tail hung like moss and vines from trees.

The second unicorn was gorgeous. Her coat was a turquoise blue, and she had a horn that seemed to be made of diamonds. Her mane and tail rippled like waves as she dared to step closer. I couldn't take my eyes off of her.

"What do you mean?" The question came out in my head, but it seemed like the other unicorns could hear me.

"We're within the ward. We're safe here, but not if you cross it, which you're about to do," another voice in my head responded. It also sounded familiar. It seemed like it was coming from the green mare.

"What's a ward?" It was like they were speaking Spanish. I had no idea what was going on.

"Think about your human self, Thea," the blue unicorn told me. *"Try it."*

I did. I thought about my old body, and quicker than I realized, I had changed back into a human. I was disappointed. My amazing experience as a unicorn was over that quickly.

Then, before I knew it, the two unicorn mares transformed in front of me. The green unicorn became Novah. The blue unicorn became Sera. All three of us were fully clothed, as if we hadn't been wearing horse hair and horns just a second ago.

I lost my mind. "What the hell!?"

I pinched myself in an attempt to wake up. But all I felt was pain, because this was real. I knew it was real. There was no denying it now.

"Thea, calm down." Sera held her hands out in front of her. "Everything's okay."

"You're a . . . I'm a . . ." I was at a loss for words.

"You transformed because you were in close proximity to us. Your magic could feel us nearby," Sera said. "Thea, you're like us."

"Like you?" I choked out. I could barely breathe. What was going on here?

Sera looked at Novah. "I think this is something we should talk about in private. Where others can't hear," she said. Novah nodded.

Sera headed back into the woods. "Come with us, Thea. We'll tell you everything."

CHAPTER 4

*A*pparently, whatever Sera had to say couldn't be said without a load of chocolate and junk food. We sat in a circle on Sera's bedroom floor, on a bunch of pillows and blankets, surrounded by chips, candy, and everything that was possibly bad for you at five a.m. Sera was playing soft music from a Bluetooth speaker, but it didn't help bring me back into reality. I couldn't stop imagining what it had felt like to gallop—actually *gallop*—through the fields near Havenwood Falls.

"I'm still waiting to wake up from this dream," I said. Novah had ripped into the Cheetos and chocolates and was eating both at once, completely unconcerned.

Sera, though, looked nervous. "You're not going to wake up. Magic is real. You experienced that today."

If she had told me that a few hours earlier, I would have thought she was crazy. But a few hours earlier, I didn't know I could grow hooves, either.

"Fine," I said. "I'm open-minded. I can believe in magic." I paused. "But I don't really understand. What am I? And what are you?"

Sera took a deep breath. "I know this might be hard to understand, but you and I, we're different from other people. You're a unicorn shifter, Thea."

"And not just any unicorn shifter," Novah said. "You're a unicorn shifter *princess*."

"Yes," Sera started. "Like us."

I stared at them for a minute. Then I burst out laughing.

"Me? Royalty?" I wiped tears away from my eyes. My gut hurt, and I had trouble breathing. Being able to transform into a unicorn, I could believe. But a princess? No way.

"It's true," Sera said indignantly. "You're the third member of the Equestriad."

"The what?" I was seriously having a hard time comprehending this stuff. "Is this what Dalton was talking about at the Burger Bar?"

"Kind of. He knows what you are. He was picking on you. He's a fae," Sera said.

"A fae? Like a faerie?" My head was spinning.

"You need to start from the beginning," Novah said with a full mouth. Sera rolled her eyes and sighed.

"First, Havenwood Falls," Sera began. "It's not like any normal town. There are all kinds of shifters here. Wolves, kelpies, bears, dragons, the list goes on. And they're not the only supernatural beings. Vampires, witches, angels—they're all here, living amongst humans in secret."

I didn't want to believe it, but my gut told me it was true. This town was just too freaky for all this shit not to be real. "Okay. Go on."

Sera played with her hair. It was seriously distracting me from the conversation. "Havenwood Falls is run by the Court of the Sun and the Moon. They protect the supernatural races here and see that our secrets are protected. Most supernaturals know about each other in Havenwood Falls, but our herd is supposed to be a secret."

"Why?" I said, baffled. "If there's a whole bunch of magical freaky people running around, what makes us special?"

Novah and Sera glanced at each other before Novah said, "Unicorns don't come from Earth. They come from a different realm, an alternate dimension named Faerie."

"You guys are really stretching my abilities to believe here." I crossed my arms. "I have a hard time thinking this isn't just one big joke."

"Everything we say is true, Thea. I promise," Sera insisted. "Within Faerie was a country called Etheria. It was a land where the unicorns roamed. It was ruled by the Equestriad—the three reigning princesses."

There was a bit of silence, and I said, "Something tells me that Etheria isn't around anymore. Otherwise, the unicorns wouldn't be here."

Sera flinched, and she said, "Well, you'd be right. For thousands of years, our foremothers before us ruled Etheria in peace and harmony, centuries upon centuries of Equestriads, passing the crown on from mother to daughter. Our mothers were the last to rule, but Etheria was destroyed on your first birthday, Thea."

"By whom?" My mind was blank.

The girls hesitated. "Her given name was Malestraude, but by the time she rose to power, the unicorns were so afraid of her that she became known as Malevolent. She's your mother, Thea."

A coldness started spreading throughout my body, starting in my gut and spreading throughout my limbs. "No. No way. My mother is Ambrosia. She raised me."

"Ambrosia was your nursemaid. Just as Novah and I were raised by our nursemaids, who we just recently found out aren't our mothers as well. All of them are unicorns, too," Sera said. "They stole us away to Earth and kept us safe while Malevolent destroyed Etheria. If she had found us, she would've killed us all."

"Ambrosia would have told me about this," I insisted stubbornly. "She wouldn't keep this from me."

"She didn't have a choice. She was forbidden by Avalar," Novah said.

"What the hell has Avalar got to do with it?" I snarled.

"He's the temporary leader of the unicorn herd," Novah said. Then as an afterthought, she muttered meekly, "And your dad."

"*What*?!" Take back what I said about the princess thing. I would think I was marrying the next British monarch far easier than I'd ever believe the jerk who'd taught me jumping today was my dad. He was unfeeling, distant . . . nothing like a father should be.

"It's true," Sera said. "I know he's not the best role model—"

"If he's my dad, why didn't he raise me instead of Ambrosia?" I shot back.

Sera and Novah glanced at each other once again anxiously before Novah said, "He thought you'd be safer with her. That's why he split us all up, just in case Malevolent got out somehow and came looking for us, or him. He brought us all back to Havenwood Falls just before we turned eighteen. It was crucial we all survive."

I was furious. It felt like my father had abandoned me. And he kinda had. Did he not want me? Was I not a good enough unicorn princess, or whatever?

Even worse, did I remind him of my mother? Was I anything like her?

My hands were shaking, but I needed to hear more of the story, so I said, "Fine. Go on."

Sera waited a few moments to make sure I was really calm before she continued. "Malevolent was part of the Equestriad, and ruled Etheria with our mothers, Iristadi and Gwenavera. Iristadi was my mother. Her last dying breath was used to make a portal to get the three of us out," Sera said firmly.

I was still calming down from the whole Avalar-is-my-dad thing. "Why do they all have such fancy long names?"

"All unicorns do," Sera said. "My real name is Seravihne, spelled like S-E-R-A-V-I-H-N-E—pronounced *Sara-veen*." She drew the word out, so I could remember it.

"And mine is Novahrynne," Novah said. "Isn't yours something flowery?"

"Aramanthe," I whispered. I'd always wondered why Ambrosia had given me such a strange name, but I just considered it unique. Now I realized she hadn't named me at all. Malestraude—Malevolent—did.

"Malevolent wanted power. She wanted to rule Etheria for herself, and not share it with her friends," Sera continued. "When her friends refused, Malevolent sold the most precious part of herself, her horn, to acquire dark magic, and used that power to kill Iristadi and Gwenavera. She was going to kill all of us, too, to secure her place on the throne permanently. She wanted to be immortal."

"Why would Avalar go against Malevolent if he helped her . . . uh . . . make me?" I asked, turning red.

"I'm not sure." Sera looked down and grimaced. "The way Mom— I mean, Lucindiana—tells it, Avalar fell in love with Malestraude, and was crushed when his mate went to the dark side. He was a knight sworn to the good of Etheria. His country came first. He got the three of us out, then started locating unicorns who came to Earth, trying to get them all to Havenwood Falls. He's spent years looking, but the herd is still small. There aren't very many of us left."

"Which brings us to our next point," Novah added. "Unicorn horns are extremely valuable. They contain powerful magic. Other supernaturals will hunt us down for them, and there aren't enough of us to fight back."

"How many unicorns are left?" I asked.

"Less than fifty or so in Havenwood Falls. If even that," Sera said.

"Jas is one of us, too. His real name is Jaspirion," Novah said. She batted her eyelashes and sighed. "Isn't that such a perfect name for a unicorn stallion?"

Sera snapped her fingers. "Novah, focus."

Novah snapped out of it. "Oh, right. But the Court's offer for us to stay in Havenwood Falls isn't permanent. They know we have beef with Malevolent. If we don't kick Malevolent's butt, the Court will kick us out of Havenwood Falls, and we'll be left to fend for ourselves," Novah said. "The Court doesn't want any trouble, and the unicorns are bringing it here. If we don't stop Malevolent now, the herd will be destroyed forever. She wants to destroy us all, out of revenge for refusing to bow to her rule. There will be no more unicorns left on Earth . . . left anywhere."

I felt the blood drain from my face. "What do you mean? She's coming here?"

"Yes." Sera's expression was grim. "Iristadi and Gwenavera fought against her, but lost. Before they died, they used their magic to imprison Malevolent in a cage of magic, forcing her to remain in Etheria."

"But the spell will fade when the next Equestriad in line is supposed to take power," Novah said. "That's your birthday, Thea. Sera and I are already eighteen. Once you come of age, Malevolent is coming for our asses. And it ain't gonna be pretty."

I swallowed nervously. "So what do we do?"

"We only have one option. We have to learn how to use our magic, so we can beat Malevolent for good," Sera said. "Novah and I have already started training, but there's so much we need you to learn, Thea. And we don't have a lot of time."

No shit. My birthday was less than four weeks away. I'd been looking forward to it, but now I was seriously dreading it.

"Are you telling me my birthday is gonna turn into one big boss battle showdown with my evil mom?" I asked.

"That's a really positive way to look at it!" Novah said in a bubbly way. I glared at her.

"We're not gonna let you do this on your own, Thea." Sera reached out and put a hand on top of mine. "We're in this together. No matter what happens."

I looked at her warm hand on mine. Her touch made me feel better, even if it was only for a moment.

I had no choice but to believe them. I was a unicorn shifter princess, my dad was Avalar, and my mom was a raging, pissed-off evil queen who was on a rampage for revenge.

And if I didn't stop her, she was going to destroy the unicorns. Permanently.

CHAPTER 5

I fell asleep at Sera's house and didn't wake up again until ten that morning. Sera and Novah were still asleep on the floor —we'd all passed out on the blankets sometime after the girls had explained everything to me.

Sera looked so pretty, with her blond hair spread all around her on the pillow. She looked like Sleeping Beauty. I resisted the urge to stare at her—you know, because I wasn't a creeper—before I headed downstairs and called Ambrosia to pick me up.

As I waited, doubt and questions ran through my mind. Ambrosia knew what was best for me. She'd been the greatest mom ever, for years.

I knew what Sera said was true. Ambrosia wouldn't have hid this from me if Avalar hadn't forced her to keep quiet.

A woman appeared in the kitchen next to the entranceway, where I was waiting. She had curly black hair and high cheekbones.

"Hello," she greeted. "I'm Lucindiana. I raised Sera. You must be Thea."

"I am," I said. "It's nice to meet you."

She looked nothing like Sera. I wondered how much of an effort it took for Sera to keep believing over the years that this was her mother.

But then again, Ambrosia didn't look anything like me, either, and I'd kept on believing the lie.

Lucindiana hesitated before she spoke. "We wanted to tell you girls," she said. "We just weren't sure of the proper time."

I didn't know what to say, so I nodded. Ambrosia pulled up, and I got in the passenger seat. It was hard for me to look at her. I didn't say much on the way home, and neither did she.

When we got home, I sat on the couch. There was a giant stuffed unicorn there—a ragged one that I'd received for my fifth birthday. I held onto it as Ambrosia sat across from me.

She handed me a plate of cookies she had made—sugar with multicolored M&M's. They were my favorite. She had made them for me after I got kicked out of Desmona Prep, as well as every time she had bad news to deliver. I dug into them, enjoying their taste. It seemed like they were the only thing left in my life that felt normal.

Ambrosia put a hand on the couch. "So now you know," she said. "We're unicorns."

My mouth was still stuffed with cookies, so I swallowed and said, "Why didn't you tell me?"

"It wasn't my place," Ambrosia said. "Avalar has authority over me."

I would never get used to this, this life of royals and class taking place in modern-day America. "Why do you care so much about what he thinks? Why do you do what he tells you to?"

"Because he risked his life to save all of us, years ago," Ambrosia responded. "My job was to keep you safe. That was the only responsibility I had."

My mouth went dry with a cookie still in it. "So you didn't care at all. You just raised me because it was your *duty*."

"No, sweetheart." Ambrosia sat next to me and put her arm around my shoulder. "I love you. I've loved you since the moment you came into this world. No matter what happens, I'll always consider you my daughter. In my heart, I'm your real mother." Her face turned menacing. "Especially compared to that vile . . . *woman*." It seemed like the nicest word she could say about my birth mother.

"Should I be afraid of her? Malevolent?" I asked.

Ambrosia's eyes flashed. "Yes, Thea. You should be, because she's very powerful." Then she shook me by the shoulders. "But don't be too afraid. Because you're stronger than she ever will be, and you have the power to beat her."

"How do you know?" I asked.

"Because each new princess that is born is passed down the powers of all the queens that have come before her," Ambrosia responded. "You were born with more magic than she has. You can defeat her."

I looked down. "I'm not so sure."

"Don't give up." Ambrosia took me gently by the chin and lifted my gaze. She brushed back my hair. "You're a princess of Etheria. It is time for you to take the crown and lead the herd. And I know you, Thea. You won't allow anyone to steal your throne, no matter who it is."

She was right. I didn't allow people to mess with me or push me around. And if the unicorns needed me . . . well, I'd be there for them. "Thanks . . . Mom."

Ambrosia's eyes were watery. She leaned forward and gave me a hug. I hugged her back and forgave her. She'd loved me and supported me in every way throughout my entire life. She really did care. It wasn't her fault that all this had happened and that she couldn't tell me who I really was.

That was Avalar's doing. And I was going to make sure he heard about it. Whatever happened, I didn't think that I could ever think of him as my dad.

Ambrosia pulled away and wiped at her eyes. "Well, I suggest you get a nap and have some lunch. You'll be meeting with Avalar soon."

"I didn't know I had a jumping lesson today," I said, confused.

"You don't. You're going to be training with your magic," Ambrosia said.

Around one o'clock, Ambrosia drove me in the direction of Havenwood Stables. But instead of stopping there, she took a dirt road deep into the forest and stopped the car after we'd driven for about ten minutes or so.

"Here we are," Ambrosia said. She pointed to a dirt path by my side, and said, "Follow that path until you reach a clearing. Avalar will be waiting for you. I'll come pick you up around five."

"Aren't you coming with me?" I asked.

Ambrosia shook her head and said, "I think it's best if you and Avalar spend some time alone. You should bond with your father."

Bonding with Avalar sounded weird and kind of gross. I didn't want him to come near me. He was a stranger. I knew he was technically my dad, but he'd been rude to me from the moment we met. He'd known I was his daughter, too, and still treated me with disgust, which only added insult to injury. I didn't want anything to do with him.

But for Ambrosia's sake, I sucked it up and said, "Okay. See you later."

I got out of the car. I felt very lonely as Ambrosia drove away and I was left in the woods alone.

At least it was a beautiful day. I hiked along the forest path, enjoying the butterflies and the sounds of birds that echoed through the forest. It was really bright out, and the sun bathed everything in a shade of yellow. It was a nice change from the clouds that had coated the area recently.

When the path ended, I entered into a circular clearing, just like Ambrosia had said. In the middle of that clearing was the silver unicorn.

The stallion from my dreams, I thought. Seeing him took my breath away. He snorted as he saw me, nostrils flaring.

I dared to come close. The unicorn stood where he was. I reached out and laid my hand on his head, stroking the area below his horn.

The unicorn snorted and breathed heavily. His black eyes gleamed. Then he transformed, and my hand was suspended in the air.

It was Avalar. The magic was totally over. I dropped my hand, and Avalar stared at me with a disapproving stare.

"You're late," he began.

I wasn't about to acknowledge that. I was a princess, wasn't I? I could be as late as I wanted to. He didn't order me around.

"You're the unicorn in my dreams," I said, astounded.

"Yes," Avalar responded dully. "I've used my magic to check up on you and make sure you were safe for years."

"Can unicorns travel through dreams?" I asked.

"They can," Avalar said. "Although that isn't useful for what we're trying to accomplish, so I suggest we focus your training on magic that is actually helpful in defeating Malevolent."

My mouth dropped open before I quickly shut it. I wasn't feeling the fatherly love here.

"First things first," Avalar began. "The Court has drawn us a ward around Havenwood Stables, where the unicorns may transform and stretch out their shifter sides. It circles around us by a mile or so. You are not to go outside the ward in your unicorn form. Ever. It is the only thing keeping you safe."

That's what Sera and Novah were talking about when they mentioned the border last night. "Will I fight Malevolent here?" I asked.

"We will attempt to lure her here to this clearing, so yes," Avalar responded. "I expect you to be able to defeat her."

"You aren't making me feel any less pressured to succeed," I stated.

"Good," he replied. "That will decrease the chances you will fail."

I really wanted to say something back, but nothing came to mind. He kinda had a point. If I didn't succeed, the unicorns were doomed, and probably Havenwood Falls with them. There was no room for error.

"To start your lesson, transform into a unicorn. Just imagine yourself taking shape," Avalar said. "Now that you know you can, it should be easy for you, like breathing."

I doubted that I could do it that easily. Yet when I thought about my unicorn form, I changed, and my body elongated and morphed to become the pink unicorn again.

Joy rushed through me. I was amazed I could still do it. I wanted to run around and kick my legs into the air, then rush off into a gallop again, but Avalar's harsh gaze made me stay put.

Avalar changed too, back into the silver stallion. For some reason, I felt like I could relate to him more when he was a unicorn rather than a human.

Avalar pointed his horn at the ground. He focused on a certain spot, and a flash of purple light came out of his horn. I jumped back, frightened by the noise it made. The purple light landed in the grass, forming a circle with strange runes I'd never seen before.

"*Magic traps,*" Avalar said as he lifted his head. "*If you can lure Malevolent into one, you can hold her within it for a time. She'll be unable to move while you do your work.*"

Avalar made it sound like a job, and not like I was trying to kill somebody. "*How am I supposed to off her? Stab her with my horn?*" I asked sarcastically.

"*A princess doesn't speak in such vile terms,*" Avalar stated. "*And no. That is not how things will be done.*"

Avalar was the type of guy who cared about stupid things, like what fork to use at dinner and what color the napkins were. He was so overly proper about everything.

"*'Kay. So I ain't gonna do that,*" I said, speaking in the worst manner possible. "*What now?*"

His nose flared. I was annoying him. "*We'll begin with the magic traps for now. Focus your attention on me. Imagine binding me to the place I stand, and put all your intent into doing so. With that intent, the magic will rise up out of your horn and force me to stand in place.*"

"*Sounds easy enough.*" But it wasn't. I tried to make the magic trap and failed. I managed to make a few purple flashes come out of my horn, but it was nothing spectacular. When I'd finally managed to make a circle on the ground around Avalar, it faded before I had the chance to really look at it. I made several more circles, but they were all gone in moments.

"Your magic is barely holding me," Avalar complained. *"You must perform the spell with force. With feeling! What you're doing now will barely contain Malevolent's hooves for a millisecond."*

"It's my first day," I replied, discouraged. *"I don't know what I'm doing. I just found out about all this!"*

"I understand time is short, but it is also of the essence," Avalar said. *"If you don't learn this magic proficiently by the time Malevolent arrives, we are most certainly done for."*

I'd had enough. I shifted back into a human and crossed my arms. Avalar changed back, and I said bluntly, "Just give it to me straight. What exactly do I have to do in order to end this thing?"

Avalar sighed. "To defeat Malevolent, you must be able to conjure the Unicorn's Lament. It is the most powerful spell known to unicornkind, and can only be performed by the Equestriad. With the spell, you, Sera, and Novah will combine your magic into one in order to take away Malevolent's magic and destroy her for good."

He then shook his head. "But Malevolent is fast, and she's deceptive. If you don't capture her in one of these magic traps and hold her in place long enough for you and your fellow princesses to perform the spell, she'll overpower all of you. You'll have to use other types of magic to wear her down before she's even weak enough to be conquered by the Lament. We will train every day, until you are ready."

This was sounding more and more impossible every minute. "If this is all so important, why didn't you bring me here to learn this stuff years ago?" I shot back at him.

"It wasn't safe. Malevolent's minions are everywhere. I had no choice," Avalar responded.

"No choice but to send me away?" I ask. "I can't believe that."

"You don't understand my motives. You're just a child," Avalar said.

"I'm not going to be a child for much longer, so tell me what to do," I said through gritted teeth.

"I cannot tell you! Only you can decide for yourself whether you are capable," Avalar said.

I curled my hands into fists. The thing was, I didn't know if I was capable of this. But I was trying my hardest, and I was fighting for a cause, and a people, that I hardly knew anything about. I was seventeen freaking years old!

"Maybe if you hadn't abandoned me as a kid, I'd be better at magic," I spat. I didn't mean to say it that way, but the words just came out.

"I didn't mean to abandon you, Thea. I can imagine why it looks that way," Avalar said.

"Looks that way? It is that way!" I shouted.

"My people—*our people*, I may remind you—come first before any personal duty to family. I have to do what's best for the herd!" Avalar roared.

"What about what's best for me? I'm your daughter!" I yelled.

I didn't wait to hear a response. I whirled around and stomped out of there before Avalar could give another condescending answer. Screw waiting for Ambrosia. I'd walk home.

I hated it, though tears burned in my eyes. I forced them to go away, though. I didn't care that I had a dad who had walked out on me, even if it was for a noble reason. I'd never needed him anyway.

I'd been just fine on my own. And if I needed to, I'd defeat Malevolent on my own.

I just didn't know how I could.

CHAPTER 6

The next day, I walked down the block to go to the gas station, because I had a craving for Cheetos. I saw Novah and Sera at the drink station, giggling and making heaven knows what.

Novah was wearing a turquoise crop top with blinged-out shorts. Sera had on a tight white shirt and a blue skirt that was big and poofy. Sera wore heels, while Novah had on high-tops. They looked like anime characters.

"What are you guys doing?" I asked, looking at the mess they had made on the counter.

"Making unicorn slurpees!" Novah said in a high-pitched, thrilled voice.

"Unicorn slurpees?" I asked, confused.

"They're the best," Novah said. "Trust me."

Novah and Sera mixed cherry and blue raspberry slushies together before they crushed up a bunch of multicolor candies, sour and sweet, pouring them into the mixture before ripping open a bag of cotton candy and placing it on top. They paid for the drinks and candy before handing one to me.

I had a bag of Cheetos in my hand, but Sera grabbed it from me and paid for it. "Here," she said. "For you."

I tried not to blush, and took a sip of the slurpee. It was packed with sugar, sour, and probably awful for you. But I loved it.

We left the gas station. Sera started by saying, "So I hope your first training session with Avalar went better than we've heard."

I shook my head, still sucking on the slurpee. I lowered my voice and looked around to make sure no one overheard us. "Nope. It was awful. I officially suck at being a unicorn."

"You don't suck," Sera said. We made our way down the street. I followed the girls, not really sure where we were going.

"I totally do." I frowned. "I couldn't even make a magic trap."

"I couldn't make a magic trap either my first day," Novah piped up. "You'll get it. Once you learn unicorn magic, it's easy to do. Unicorns are natural spellcasters."

I wasn't so sure. The girls knocked on the door of a little bungalow house and waited.

"Why are we here?" I asked, looking around.

"Every shifter is required by the Court to get a tattoo, for security purposes," Sera said. "Addie does them. She's a witch, and you're next. Ambrosia got hers yesterday."

"What!" I yelped. I was totally afraid of needles.

"We got ours." Novah showed me her tattoo, one of a horseshoe with an exploding star in the middle.

"Where'd you get yours?" I asked Sera nervously.

Sera wiggled her eyebrows. Then she pulled down the top of her skirt ever so slightly, to show a unicorn head in rainbow colors tattooed on her ass.

"Sera!" I hissed, then giggled obnoxiously. "You didn't!"

"I totally did." She grinned as she pulled up her skirt. "Where do you want yours?"

I wasn't sure. I didn't even know what to get. "Has this been paid for?"

"Avalar took care of it," Sera said. She dragged me toward the house. "Come on!"

I wondered what Avalar had as his tattoo. Probably a frowny face, or the word NO written in big red letters.

A woman opened the door. She was young, with tattoos, piercings, and ripped up jeans. She intimidated me a little.

"Hi, Addie." Sera beamed, and her smile made my heart skip. "We've brought her."

"Thea, right?" Addie asked, and I nodded. She gestured for me to come inside. "Let's get you started."

I decided on a tattoo of a galloping unicorn in color on my shoulder. It was smaller than the size of my hand. The needles didn't hurt as much as I thought they would, but I still held Novah's and Sera's hands like I was giving birth while getting it.

"I love your tattoos," I told Addie as she finished up my own ink.

Addie smiled. "Thanks. A lot of them are for decoration, and not necessarily magical purposes."

"So why do I need this tattoo, anyway?" I asked.

"Your tattoo is a part of the Registry for supernatural creatures in town," Addie explained. "The ink has magic within it. The tattoos connect with the protective wards around Havenwood Falls. Kylo Ren, get down."

Addie pushed her tuxedo cat off the table next to us and got to work cleaning my new tattoo. As a witch, Addie had four familiars, all named after Star Wars characters. I liked pets, and Addie had so many; besides Kylo Ren, she also had Chewie, a wolf, Skywalker, a raven, and Princess Leia, a miniature dragon. I thought that the dragon was the most amazing.

I kinda hated Star Wars, but I didn't tell Addie that, because I thought it would offend her, and it wouldn't be smart to piss off a witch. I was a novice unicorn, and I was pretty sure in a fight, she'd win.

When we waved goodbye to Addie, I felt more confident. For some reason, just getting a tattoo made me feel like a part of this town —not just someone who was supposed to save it.

The three of us walked back to the gas station and got into Sera's car, and she drove us out of town. She parked near the stables. We sat in the truck bed and shared the Cheetos as I complained about Avalar.

"I just don't think I'm cut out for this, guys." I leaned against the truck and looked up at the clear blue sky. "I'm supposed to be this awesome unicorn princess that's full of power, but I can't even cast a simple spell. Plus, lately, I can't stop eating."

"Same, girl. It's stress," Novah said. A Cheeto popped out of her mouth, and I laughed.

Sera stood up in the truck bed. "The protective wards around the stables aren't far from here. Let's practice. I bet you aren't as terrible as you think."

"Girl, you're in heels and a skirt. You can't hike through the woods," Novah said skeptically.

Sera shrugged. She pulled off her heels and tossed them before jumping down into the mud, not caring if her feet got dirty. "No time like the present."

My stomach wiggled. Sera was so adventurous. I really liked that about her.

"Ugh . . . fine." Novah stood up, too, and I had no choice but to follow. We walked until we hit the boundary line for the ward, then we transformed. I followed Sera and Novah through the forest as a unicorn until we reached the same clearing I'd been practicing in with Avalar yesterday.

Sera turned toward me. *"Okay, Thea, show us what you've got."*

I tried. I attempted to make a magic trap, but all that came out of my horn was purple smoke.

"This is pointless." I stomped my hoof in frustration. I'd never get it.

"Don't give up. Try a different way," Sera offered.

"Yes. Imagine fixating a person to one spot, like glue," Novah said.

I tried again. I pointed my horn at Novah and imagined that she was stuck in a giant, sticky vat of glue. A purple shot flew out of my horn and made a circle on the ground with the strange runes again.

"Hey! I can't move!" Novah squealed. Sera laughed, and the sound was like jingling bells.

"I did it!" I cheered.

Sera danced on her hooves, like she was clapping. *"Well done! Do it again!"*

Sera and Novah were way easier to practice with than Avalar. I picked up the magic trap within ten minutes with them teaching me and had mastered it within twenty.

"*Show me more!*" I demanded. Now that Avalar wasn't around, the pressure was off, and I was actually getting excited about magic.

"*Try this. It's an offensive maneuver. Imagine focusing all your magic as a weapon, like shooting a water gun.*" Sera bowed her head, and a blue light shot out of her horn this time. It surrounded me and felt like a dozen feathers tickling against my sides.

"*Hey! That tickles!*" I laughed. Sera withdrew her horn, and the tickling went away.

"*It wouldn't tickle if I didn't want it to. It'd really hurt if I wished it,*" Sera said. "*Unicorn magic is all about your intention. If you can think it, you can do it. Watch.*"

She pointed her horn at a tree, and another blue blast came out of it. It hit the tree, and what was left behind was a large, sizzling black spot in the trunk that was still burning.

"*Woah,*" I said. I tried to copy her, and although the blast was smaller, I was still able to copy the spell. I left a tiny black burn spot in the trunk of the tree, right above Sera's.

I turned my head toward Novah instead and imagined her surrounded by bubbles. As I thought of the image in my head, bubbles began sprouting out of my horn. They surrounded Novah, hundreds of them, and she snickered as she popped them with her horn.

"*You're getting it,*" Sera encouraged, and I felt myself swell with pride. I was feeling much more confident.

"*Is there any more?*" I asked eagerly.

"*That's all we know,*" Novah said. "*Avalar didn't teach us much. He wanted to wait for you.*"

"*Has he taught you the Unicorn's Lament?*" I asked them.

Sera shook her head. "*Avalar was waiting to practice it until the three of us were together.*"

That was a disappointment. I was hoping the girls could teach me, instead of Avalar. They made it fun.

"*We should go back. Avalar warned us not to stretch our magic too far,*" Sera said.

We headed back, changing at the ward boundary. On the way back to her truck, I said, "You really seem to respect Avalar."

"He's the leader of the Etherian herd," Sera said. "At least he is for now, until the three of us take over. He's sacrificed a lot to make sure the unicorns don't go extinct."

"He's not easy to get along with," I pointed out.

"He just wants us to succeed. He has to push us. He doesn't have a choice," Sera said.

When we got back to Sera's truck, Novah was patting her face down, trying to wipe the sweat that was on her forehead with her shirt.

"Ugh. I *so* need a facial," Novah complained. She acted like she was wilting.

"Agreed. We're having a spa day, tonight," Sera said. "It's the only way to get rid of all this stress."

"Mani-pedis and veggie pizza!" Novah sang out.

"And makeovers, too," Sera said, and she looked at me. "I got a new makeup kit I've been dying to try out, Thea. I'd love to make you feel more relaxed."

"Oh, um, sure," I said. I got tongue-tied, and the words came out kind of slurred, but if Sera noticed, she didn't say anything. She just smiled at me.

Was it just me, or did her words seem to imply something more? She held my gaze, and I felt myself getting hot all over.

"I totally need this," Novah groaned, and the spell was broken as Sera tore her gaze away. "I need to vent about guys."

"You always need help with guys," Sera said.

Novah flipped her off before she added, "By the way, are we watching our show tonight?"

"The one with the ponies? Absolutely," Sera said, and Novah squealed. I was pretty sure the show they were talking about was a cartoon made for a much younger audience, but I didn't care . . . because I secretly loved it, too.

Sera and Novah acted so girly. They were always feminine, all the time. I don't think I ever saw them wear jeans. It reminded me of how I used to be, before the fire. I missed that.

But at the same time, I didn't think I could ever return to being that person—the girl I used to be. She was dead. She'd died in the flames.

Still, mani-pedis and veggie pizza sounded amazing right now. Especially since it was at Sera's house.

"I'm in," I said.

Sera wrapped her arm around my waist. "I didn't know you had a choice," she said playfully, and she shook me.

My heart stumbled as I felt her tight hold around my hips. When she touched me, it felt . . . amazing. A warmth started in my chest and spread throughout my entire body. What she'd said had more weight than she could ever know.

Nope. My feelings had been spoken for, and there was no turning back now, not even if I wanted to. I already knew I could try to make myself like someone else, and it wouldn't work. I'd only known Sera for two days, yet that was all it took. I didn't believe in love at first sight before I got to Havenwood Falls, but I did now.

When it came to Sera, there was no choice involved whatsoever.

CHAPTER 7

wo weeks passed so quickly in Havenwood Falls I didn't realize my birthday was only a few days away until I looked at the calendar.

I started school at Havenwood Falls High on August 21, along with Sera and Novah. I thought it was a normal high school, until I found that it was packed with supernaturals mixed in among the unknowing humans. The classes were pretty normal. Sera told me there was a Sun and Moon Academy for supernaturals in the town that was kept completely under wraps from the non-magical community. They offered magical classes, which I was interested in taking, but Sera told me that the three of us weren't allowed to attend until after we defeated Malevolent, as Avalar wanted all of our attention focused on the task at hand.

I wasn't surprised. Avalar ruined everything.

My favorite class was Art, which was taught by Mr. Weaver. He was a fairly young teacher who seemed enthusiastic and excited about starting a new semester. I instantly liked him, even when my painting didn't turn out quite right. He said it looked beautiful even though I was certain it looked like shit. I think it needed more glitter. At the same time, I was a unicorn, so *everything* could always use more glitter. Weaver gave me an A anyway.

At the same time, there seemed something spooky about him, but I couldn't quite put my finger on what. I wondered if he was supernatural, too, but didn't have the balls to ask.

While at lunch, I spotted a beautiful girl with a body like a supermodel. It took one look at her gold-flecked eyes to see that she was a supernatural.

I was surprised when Sera and Novah made a beeline for her and sat at her table. I didn't know what else to do, so I followed their lead.

"Thea, I'd like you to meet Miranda Saunders," Sera said as we sat down. "Havenwood Falls High's resident sassy and fearless chick." Sera leaned in and whispered under her breath, "She's a vampire."

Miranda flashed me a smile. I thought I saw a glimpse of fangs, but I could have been imagining things. "Well, hello there, Thea. The girls have told me so much about you."

"You guys have been talking about me?" I asked Sera, raising an eyebrow.

"Only like, a bit," Novah confessed. I rolled my eyes.

Miranda dropped her voice to a whisper and leaned in. "Don't worry about me, little unicorn. I don't bite." She laughed. "Much. I'm a bit of a *unicorn*, too. One of a kind."

She winked at me, and I didn't quite get what she meant. But whatever. It seemed like the more secrets you uncovered in this town, the more you had to discover.

"Miranda's great," Sera said. "You want to know the latest fashion, you go to her."

"Yeah, when she's not drooling over Kai Reynolds," Novah teased. Miranda reached across the table and smacked Novah on the shoulder.

I noticed a designer purse sitting on the table in front of Miranda that I was dying to have. The girl had a great sense of style. I wanted to raid her closet *so* badly.

"Fan of labels?" Miranda asked me, wiggling her eyebrows.

"Yes," I confessed. "Though I don't really have the extra cash to spend." I blushed.

"We'll go shopping sometime," Miranda said. "I know how to get some great deals."

I relaxed. For a vampire, Miranda was actually pretty nice. Havenwood Falls High was a lot more welcoming than most of the other schools I'd been to. Especially the last one. I had a feeling I'd fit right in here.

Despite us having to go to school, Avalar trained us every day. Thankfully, he'd moved on to group sessions, training all of us at once as opposed to working with me one-on-one. I was better with the girls around, but I still couldn't seem to conquer my powers unless Avalar wasn't there and either Sera or Novah were teaching me. I felt too pressured to succeed when Avalar was watching me, and I couldn't take the disappointed look in his eyes every time I failed to perform a spell. Clearly, I wasn't the daughter he'd been hoping for.

We didn't get a lot of time to ride horses, which made me kinda grumpy. The few rides we got were scattered here and there around our training, and Avalar limited our time with the horses because he wanted us to focus on beating Malevolent.

I personally thought riding would help me de-stress about the whole thing and make my magic better, but I didn't speak up, mostly because I was too afraid to. Voicing my opinion had been beaten out of me at Desmona Prep, and it was a habit I found hard to break.

Still, it was nice the few chances we did get to ride. Like on the Saturday before my birthday, which was August 31.

"Can you believe we're going to be facing Malevolent a week from today?" Novah asked. Her usual cheery tone was there, but it was tainted with a bit of fear. She, Sera, and I had snuck the horses out of the stables and were riding them in the farthest pasture from the barn, where hopefully Avalar wouldn't see. Novah and I were watching Sera fly over the jumps while we waited for our turns.

"It doesn't feel real," I responded. I kept my eyes on Sera as she sailed over the jumps. As long as I kept my eyes on her, I was calm.

"It doesn't." Novah shook her head. "Are you nervous?"

I nodded. "I'm not really afraid of Malevolent, though."

And I wasn't. She was scary to think about, in a way, but I wasn't terrified of her. I didn't know if that was because I was foolish, or because I didn't know what I was truly up against.

"Really?" Novah was surprised. "Then what are you afraid of?"

I didn't hesitate to answer. "Of failing. I want to prove myself. I want to show these people that I can lead them."

Avalar had introduced me to the rest of the herd, and he hadn't been lying when he said it was small. Most of them had been at that barbecue Sera had taken us to. So many unicorns came up and thanked me personally for saving them, and defeating Malevolent, though I hadn't yet done anything but train.

I didn't want to let them down. If they died by Malevolent's horn, their deaths were on my hands.

"You aren't going to fail. None of us are," Novah said.

"How can you be so sure?"

"I am." Novah looked at me. "I know we can do this, as long as it's together."

I didn't answer. I was too busy watching Sera effortlessly finish the course.

Novah reached across and nudged me. "Someone's got a crush on Sera."

My cheeks and ears immediately burned. "What! No, I don't!"

"You do," Novah teased. "Why don't you ask her out already? It's getting old watching you pine over her."

"She probably doesn't even like girls," I mumbled.

"She likes you," Novah said. "She told me so."

I wanted to do backflips on my horse. "You're not making it up?"

"Why would I make something like that up?" Novah asked.

Sera came back from finishing the course. Novah urged his horse forward to take his turn, and Sera stood her Thoroughbred beside my Arabian. My hands were shaking. Why not ask now?

"Hey, Sera?" I asked.

"Yes?" She looked at me, and I almost lost my courage. Ransom sensed my nervousness and danced underneath me. I had to pull on the reins to get him to stand still.

"After this, do you want to . . . go out tonight?" I asked.

"Like on a date?" Sera batted her eyelashes.

I forced myself to pick my jaw off the ground. "Um, yeah. I mean, no. Unless you want it to be, that is." *I screwed that up.*

She gave me a smile and said, "It's a date. Pick me up at seven."

Novah came back from her course. I urged my horse forward, and we flew over all the jumps. I felt so confident and elated. It was like I was flying. I was going on a date with Sera tonight!

But by the time I got back to my house later to take a nap, I was freaking out. I didn't know what to do. I'd had crushes on girls, but I'd never asked one out before on an official date. My nap ended up being nonexistent as I tossed and turned, wondering if Sera liked me too.

Ambrosia was so excited when she came home from work and I told her about the date. She spent the entire evening helping me get ready. By the time she was done with me, my hair was curled and I was wearing a brand-new dress, decorated with multicolor florals, along with heels and a pearl necklace.

I swallowed as I saw my reflection in the mirror. I hadn't dressed like this in a really long time. Maybe things could be different now, in Havenwood Falls.

Before Ambrosia took me to Sera's house, she dropped me off at Fairy Tale Florists. I couldn't decide what kind of flowers Sera would like best, so I just went with a bouquet made of irises and forget-me-nots, because they matched the color of her pelt.

When Sera answered the door, my heart skipped a beat. She looked amazing. Her hair was in a high ponytail with a bunch of curls, and she had on a lacy blue dress with exposed shoulders and a tea-length skirt.

She squealed when she saw the flowers. "Oh my gosh! They're amazing, Thea."

She leaned over and kissed me on the cheek as she took the flowers from me. My entire body glowed. She walked inside her kitchen and put the flowers in a vase before she joined me on the porch.

Ambrosia waved goodbye. "Have fun, you two!"

She drove away, and I turned to Sera.

"You'll probably have to drive," I said, a bit embarrassed. "Seeing as how I don't have a car."

Sera jingled her keys at me. "Fine by me. I like taking the wheel in relationships."

Despite the bad pun, I couldn't stop my insides from flip-flopping. Sera implied that we could be something more.

We hopped in her truck, and Sera started up the engine. "So, where are we off to?" she asked, looking at me.

"Um . . ." I was the one who asked, so I should've come up with a plan on where to take her. I was really bad at this.

Noticing my blank expression, Sera laughed and said, "That's okay. I really wanted Chinese, if that's cool with you?"

Sera could want to eat dirt, and it'd be cool with me. "That actually sounds really good," I said. "Let's go."

She parked at Miller's Plaza, and we walked into Sakura Buffet. When we went inside, it was pretty full, as it was a Saturday night. We managed to get a small booth at the back, but instead of sitting on the other side like she was supposed to, she sat next to me. Sera pressed herself up against my body in the booth, and I went lightheaded. I could barely talk as the waiter handed us the menus.

I decided on the deluxe stir-fried vegetables, and Sera ordered veggie lo mein.

When the waiter was gone, I turned to Sera with an apologetic smile. "Sorry. I'm not an expert on this dating thing. I've never taken another girl out on a date before."

"That's okay." Sera reached under the table and interwove her fingers with mine, clasping our hands tightly together. "I've never been on a date with another girl, either."

Her skin was soft and warm—nothing like holding a guy's hand. I looked at her manicured fingernails on top of my hand and thought that I'd never been happier in my entire life.

We held hands the entire time until our food showed up. We didn't really say much, but Sera rested her head on my shoulder and leaned into me even more than she already was. I knew we were cuddling in view of the entire restaurant, but I didn't care what people thought. I bet we looked really cute together.

Only when food was on the table did Sera loosen her grip from mine. After dinner, she took me to this crazy bookstore called Into the Mystic New Age Books and Gifts. She talked about crystals and yoga, and showed me all these books about magic and reaching your inner potential. She was really into this psychic stuff. She told me she took yoga classes at NamaStays Inn, and wanted to know if I'd like to come to her next class . . . after Malevolent was defeated.

I obviously said yes immediately. Watching Sera do yoga sounded like heaven. If I didn't have a good enough motive to survive before, I did now.

When we were done at the bookstore, after Sera had practically bought the place out, she noticed I was carrying a small bag, too.

"What's that you got?" she asked curiously when we hopped back in her truck.

I hesitated. It was supposed to be a surprise, but she had already seen.

"It's for you." I took it out of the bag. It was a crystal pendant on a necklace, blue and pink in color. The colors mingled together and made a beautiful pattern within the crystal. "It reminded me of us."

I looped it around her neck and fastened it. We were so close in her truck our faces were almost touching, and there wasn't a lot of space to move around.

Sera lifted her face so that her lips were only centimeters away from mine.

"Do you believe in fairy tales?" she whispered. Then she leaned forward and kissed me.

I didn't expect the kiss, so I was surprised. I sat there in shock for a moment, trying to process that my dreams were coming true, before I realized that I should probably kiss her back. I closed my eyes and placed my hands on her lap as I kissed her, feeling fireworks explode in my chest.

Kissing a girl was a lot different from kissing a guy. Sera was soft, she smelled good, and she was gentle. She went slow. Her lips felt like velvet against mine as she moved them. Her mouth is smaller, and she didn't bite or suck on my lip like guys did, or be aggressive. Instead, she acted like my mouth was something to treat with the most tender care. She was in no rush to go further, but instead drew out the kiss like it was the best kiss she'd ever had in her life. Her hands lifted to part back the curls from my face, and I felt like I was in heaven. I didn't have to tell her how far to go, or to stop, because it was like she was naturally attentive to my needs and just knew.

It was kind of cheesy, but as I kissed Sera, I felt . . . sparkly. Just sparkles, everywhere. I felt like my body was going to start projecting rainbows. It was a very unicorn way of putting things.

When Sera pulled away, she looked shy. It was a weird look on her. She wasn't a shy person. She was always brave.

"I've never kissed a girl before, either," Sera confessed.

"Me neither."

I blinked at her, and she put her hands on the wheel. "Come on. I want to show you something."

Sera drove until we stopped at Town Square Park. She held my hand again and pulled me along to a large wooden gazebo at the southeast corner of the park. When we stepped inside the gazebo, Sera began playing a song on her phone. She took my hands in hers, and we started slow-dancing to the tune that was playing low in the background.

"What is this place?" I asked.

"It's my favorite place in all of Havenwood Falls," Sera said. She spun me around before she drew me in, even closer this time. "I thought that when I found someone I liked, I'd bring them here, and we could dance."

"I didn't know you liked me." I looked downward. "I thought you would laugh at me when I asked you out," I confessed.

Sera stared at me and said, "If you thought I would laugh when you asked me on a date, you don't know me very well."

"I didn't back then," I said. I wrapped my arms tighter around her waist. "I know you now."

I kissed her this time. The way we held each other when we kissed again was like nothing I'd ever experienced. It was like being embraced by a cloud, and I could tell Sera would never hurt me. She was so sensitive to my needs it almost made me emotional.

When Sera pulled away, she said, "I changed my mind. You're the best part of Havenwood Falls."

I smiled and continued swaying us to the music. I didn't know how to respond to that. Probably because it made me too choked up.

"How did you end up in Havenwood Falls?" Sera said. "Obviously Avalar summoned you here, but where did you grow up?"

The happy moment faded, and the cloud of joy lifted. I cleared my throat and frowned.

"It all began two years ago," I said. "Ambrosia had this great job, and we lived in this huge house in New Orleans. Life was so perfect."

Tears were starting to dot my eyelashes. I really didn't want to cry in front of Sera. "Then our house caught fire one day. The gas line wasn't hooked up to the stove correctly, or something stupid like that. Ambrosia and I got out okay, but we lost everything, and the hospital she worked for had massive budget cuts and she ended up losing her job. We had to live off the insurance money. I had to quit riding lessons, and Ambrosia couldn't find work. We were so poor."

"That's so terrible." Sera reached out and brushed away a tear that fell down my cheek that I didn't even know was there.

"After the fire, I was angry. I'd always had daddy issues." I shook my head. "Ambrosia told me my dad had left when I was a baby. I didn't understand why he would just run off on me and Ambrosia like that. And after the fire, after we lost everything, I couldn't handle it. I ended up getting in trouble, and the judge sentenced me to a year at Desmona Prep. It was a school for troubled kids outside New Orleans. It had a great riding program, but that was the only good thing about it. I got picked on a lot there."

"That's horrible." Sera seemed shocked.

"It was pretty bad." I had trouble meeting her eyes. "I was a girly girl growing up. Pink was my favorite color. I loved dresses and doing my hair and makeup. Bows, pearls—they were my favorite. I liked ponies and watching rom-coms and reading love stories."

My voice was getting wobbly. "But at Desmona Prep, anything feminine was considered a weakness. They made boys and girls wear the same uniforms and didn't separate anything based on gender. At first, I thought it was a good thing, because it helped make us all feel equal, but at the same time, I felt like they pushed masculinity over femininity. Romance novels were banned. They were considered a lower class of literature. They didn't allow dances or parties. No one was allowed to dress up or accessorize, even on the weekends when we could wear our normal clothes. Everyone was forced to wear T-shirts and jeans. If you acted like a girl in any way, you were a target."

I looked down. "I had the girliness beat out of me by bullies. And criticized out of me by teachers. So I kind of learned that being a woman was considered weak."

"Being feminine isn't a weakness," Sera argued. "It's actually harder to be soft and kind than it is to be harsh and tough, especially in this world."

"I know that now. You taught me." I leaned upward and kissed her forehead. "And I am really tired of pretending to be something I'm not."

"I'm so sorry that happened to you," Sera said. I could tell she truly meant it.

I shrugged. "It was what happened. I'm past it now."

Sera's expression was doubtful when I said that. "I grew up in Louisiana too. I had a pretty great life. I was always popular."

"I can imagine that." I pictured Sera, lounging on Florida beaches with tons of popular preps around. She was so nice and sweet, so extroverted and so pretty, that I bet people flocked to her. She'd never been an outcast like me.

"I never really went through anything tragic," Sera said. "I came to Havenwood Falls last year, along with Novah. We didn't know we were unicorns until we shifted together the first time we met at the stables. It was a pretty big shock. We were just as surprised as you were, at the beginning."

I nodded. "It's hard to know you've been lied to all your life."

"Right. But honestly, it was more of a relief than anything. There was a part of me I felt like had been hiding my entire life. Then it came out once I became a unicorn."

"Me too," I confessed. "Even though this is all crazy new to me, knowing about this world actually makes me feel better. I always knew in my heart there was something more. I just couldn't put my finger on what."

Sera frowned. "I just wish I could've met my parents. Novah feels the same way. We have names, but don't know anything else about them. Neither one of us have asked much, because we don't want to upset our adoptive moms. You're lucky that your parents are still alive, Thea. Even if your mother is totally evil."

"Avalar isn't exactly an outstanding father," I mumbled.

"No. But at least he's alive," she whispered.

"Your friends probably made up for his absence." Now that I had Avalar in my life, I was quickly learning fathers weren't all they were cracked up to be.

She shrugged. "I had a lot of friends growing up . . . a lot of boyfriends, too . . . but it always felt like something was . . . missing." She brushed my cheek lightly with her hand, and cupped the side of my face. "I didn't know what was missing was you."

My heart melted. I brought her in close for a really tight hug—you know, the kind that crushes you to another person and makes you feel like you're one.

"Thea," Sera started, and her lips moved against my ear as she whispered. "Ever since I found the Equestriad, I feel whole. Being a unicorn is what I've been meant to do my entire life. I won't be able to stand it if Malevolent takes that away from me."

I nestled my face in her ponytail, and made myself a promise. I was going to defeat Malevolent. For Sera's sake as much as mine.

CHAPTER 8

I'd learned in the past month there was nothing unicorns loved more than sugar— and there was a coffee shop in town that apparently made the best drink ever, according to Sera and Novah. Even better, it was named after us—though I didn't really buy that from the girls.

Coffee Haven was owned by a gorgeous woman named Willow with a petite build and amazing turquoise eyes. It took a lot for me to rip my gaze away from her. Like, seriously, if I was a few years older, I'd be all over that. If I didn't know I already liked girls, Willow would've made me realize.

Sera and Novah forced me to order a drink called Unicorn Farts. I thought the name was kind of dumb (and a bit gross). Like, really, you don't want to see my farts, because they're disgusting. But at the first sip, I fell in love. This seriously was going to be my new favorite thing.

Willow smiled at me as I sipped. "Good?"

"Very." I was downing it in seconds. "I'd love another."

Willow laughed. "Coming right up." She paused, and then added, "Don't worry. I know you're nervous, but whatever it's about, I'm sure it'll all work out. It usually does."

She gave me a smile before continuing to make my drink. I was standing there speechless with my mouth hanging open. What did she just say?

"Willow is an empath." Sera leaned over, whispering to me. "She can read emotions."

Did everyone in this town have crazy magical powers? It was kinda hard to get used to. I figured I'd meet an alien on the street next. Sera and Novah placed the same order before we started the walk down the street to Jas's house, who was having an end-of-summer pool party.

There were only five days left until Malevolent would arrive, and all of us were starting to freak out. We'd mastered as many spells as we could, but Avalar still hadn't taught us the Unicorn's Lament—which he promised he was going to do this week.

"Hey, lovebirds," Jas said as we arrived, giving a pointed look at me and Sera. There were already a ton of unicorn shifters in the pool, and he was at the grill, cooking veggie dogs.

I blushed, but Sera said back playfully, "You're just pissed you can't get between this, Jas." She gestured between me and her.

"Right you are," Jas said, and he gave us a wink. "Though I think the chances are slim in that department."

Sera giggled, and I said nothing. We weren't officially girlfriends yet, but that was because I'd been too nervous to ask Sera, and it had become pretty clear she wanted me to ask her out first. We'd kissed a few more times, but since Novah was usually with us, we kept the PDA to a minimum.

Novah took her opportunity to slink up to Jas's side and wrap an arm around his waist. "How you doing today, Jas?"

"Oh, just fine, darlin'." Jas bent down and kissed Novah's forehead. She gave a girly squeal, and hopped up and down. Sera made a gagging sound, and I rolled my eyes.

"Like you two are any better," Novah shot at us. I snickered.

I stayed at the pool party until night fell, and Sera wanted to go. We left Novah with Jas. She was sitting on his lap in a lawn recliner and obviously didn't even notice we were leaving.

Sera had been in a good mood at the party, but when we left she seemed kinda . . . upset.

"What's wrong?" I asked her as we walked toward her truck. "You look troubled."

Sera paused for a moment, before she said, "Avalar didn't want me to tell you this, but the Court warned him that if we can't deal with Malevolent, they'll go outside the town wards to defeat her themselves. If she hurts or kills anyone, or exposes the supes to humans, the Court will end up kicking all the unicorns out of Havenwood Falls. He told me because he thought I could handle it." Sera sighed. "The thing is, I don't think I can."

"Why didn't he say anything to me?"

"He didn't want to make you feel more pressured than you already are," Sera explained. "He knows he's been pushing you harder than Novah and me."

Avalar cared about my well-being? That was a first.

"We're going to win," I told Sera. "I know we are."

"I hope so." Sera stopped at the ward line for the unicorns. "You wanna go for a run?"

I longed to stretch my unicorn legs. "Sure."

We entered into the woods, and once we were in the cover of the trees, Sera and I changed. We ran freely through the forest like unicorns were meant to do, and I enjoyed the feel of the sunset shining down on my back, and the flash of Sera's hooves as she ran in front of me.

But it wasn't enough. In the past month, Sera, Novah, and I had galloped all around this ward, and I'd already seen everything in the area. I wanted more. I wanted to explore.

At nightfall, I stopped at the edge of a known border, and shifted back. Sera changed beside me, and I said, "What is it with the dumb boundary, anyhow? Why can't we cross it?"

"Thea, it's not safe," Sera repeated. "The Court set up the ward so we can change, but Avalar's magic isn't able to extend out that far. He set up protective boundaries that nobody but unicorns can cross within the ward. If we go outside of that, we're unprotected."

I rolled my eyes. "If it's a vampire, we can just stab it with our horns or something."

"It doesn't work like that in Havenwood Falls. Thea, you're too curious," Sera said nervously.

I gave a mischievous grin. "I just like a bit of excitement. Catch me if you can!"

"Thea!"

I had already changed back and was galloping through the woods over the boundary line before Sera had even shifted, giving me a good head start.

I heard Sera's hooves behind me and laughed. This was so much fun. I liked the thrill of the chase. *"You've gotta be faster than that, slowpoke!"* I laughed.

"Thea, this isn't funny!" Sera's voice was panicked. What was she so worried about?

Then the area grew darker. It was like the light of the moon went away, and the stars vanished. I could barely see. My breathing became ragged, and my heartbeat was so loud, I could hear it in my ears. I slowed to a halt, and Sera came up beside me.

"What's going on?" Even in my head, I sounded out of breath.

Sera didn't answer. *"We have to get back to the boundary line."* There was an edge of fear to her voice.

I heard growls. Barks. And howls. Out of the shadows stepped wolves, a whole pack of them, all black in color, with red eyes that glowed in the darkness.

I was freaking out. *"I thought the pack wasn't allowed around the stables?"* I asked, frightened.

"They're not Havenwood Falls shifters! They're Malevolent's minions!" Sera shouted. *"She's getting more powerful! It won't be long before she can break out of her cage! Run, Thea, run!"*

I turned on my hind legs and bolted back in the direction of the boundary line, but it was dark, and I had lost my way. Sera was right behind me. The wolves chased us through the bushes, and got closer and closer. I could feel their hot breaths on my hooves.

I was faster than Sera, and at the moment, all I wanted was to get the wolves away from her. I galloped as hard as I could, breaking away from her and leading the wolves in a different direction.

"Thea, don't!" Sera's cry was lost to the wind as I led the wolves away from her. I jumped over fallen logs and rocks in my way, galloping through a river, but nothing stopped or slowed down the wolves, and I was getting tired. They started approaching me from all sides, surrounding me.

I aimed a kick at one of the wolves. It hit true, but instead of dealing a powerful blow to the wolf's body, all it did was go right through.

It hit me. The wolves were made of magic. Malevolent's dark magic. I couldn't touch them, but they could hurt me.

One of the wolves jumped and sank his teeth into my flank. I gave a cry of pain, and two more wolves latched onto my ankles. I went down, and the whole pack of them jumped onto my body, sinking their teeth into my flesh and tearing with all their strength.

Blood gushed out of the wounds, and I realized that I couldn't get up. The wolves were too heavy, and there were too many of them. I tried to fight back, but my hooves and horn went through smoke.

I felt weak as my blood pooled around me. I was dying. There was no way out of this.

"Thea, no!" There was a blinding, flashing light, one I realized came from Sera's horn. The great light seemed to burn the wolves on impact, and they howled with pain. They ran away from me as Sera came galloping near.

"Sera," I thought, just before I passed out. I saw a white, healing light glow from Sera's horn, and felt my broken flesh knit together as the world vanished around me.

CHAPTER 9

When I woke up, I was lying on my couch at home, a group of figures around me. As the room became clearer, I recognized faces. The Equestriad. Ambrosia. And Avalar.

Who looked pretty pissed.

"What were you thinking?" he demanded.

Sera had tear stains on her face, and her nose was pink.

"What happened?" I asked blearily.

"Sera healed you and brought you back home. You could've been killed," Avalar said through clenched teeth.

A rush of anger went through me. "I know that would've been a tragedy, seeing as how you still need me to do your dirty work," I spat.

"Thea, that's enough," Ambrosia snapped. She rarely got angry, but she was furious now. "You made a reckless, childish decision. You put yourself and Sera in terrible danger."

I fell silent. I knew when to shut up.

"Do you realize what you nearly jeopardized?" Avalar bellowed. "Years of preparation were almost ruined!"

"I get it," I said sourly. "You could at least be happy that I'm still alive."

Avalar looked surprised. "I . . . I am glad," he stated. "I'm relieved to see that you're unharmed. But that's no excuse for your behavior."

"I'm sorry," I said, though it was more to Sera than to him. Watching her cry felt worse than the wolves' teeth in me had.

Avalar straightened up. "Rest. I expect the three of you to arrive in the clearing at dawn. Tomorrow, we work on the Unicorn's Lament."

Avalar stomped out. He slammed the door, which seemed out of character for him. I'd never seen him truly lose his temper before.

Ambrosia's harsh glare vanished when he was out of her sight. "I'm very upset with you," she said, stroking my hair back. "But I'm so grateful you're alive. Those wolves could've torn you apart."

Sera ran out, covering her face and heading into my room. Novah looked at me and thumbed her hand in the direction she'd gone. "You'd better go handle that."

A pit of guilt settled in my stomach. I slowly got off the couch, but I found I didn't feel sore, dizzy, or disoriented. Sera's healing magic had made me as good as new.

Horrid terror wrapped itself around me as I remembered what had happened. Those wolves weren't even the worst of it. They were Malevolent's minions. Those were her lackeys. She had to be a million times more powerful. How could we stand up to that?

I entered my bedroom. Sera was sitting on my bed, clutching a pillow and crying into it.

I sat beside her. I wanted to touch her, but I figured I should keep my hands to myself right now. "Sera, I'm so sorry," I started. "I should've listened to you. We had no business going over the boundary line."

"It was stupid," Sera snapped.

"I agree that what I did was stupid," I said. "It never should've happened."

Sera's lip quivered. "You don't understand. You could've been killed. If I hadn't been able to heal you—"

She got off the bed. She crossed her arms and whipped around, turning her back to me.

"Hey." I got up. I turned her back around to face me, though it was hard to do, because tears were streaming down her face. "I really am sorry, Sera. I am so, so sorry." I was crying now, too, because I couldn't watch Sera bawl for long without it giving me some sort of waterworks.

"I was watching them rip you apart and hoping I could get to you in time." Sera's voice was muddled with tears. "Do you know how awful that is?"

I tried to picture myself in Sera's position and couldn't, because the thought of her being devoured by wolves was too hard to handle. "I can't even imagine. But thank you for saving me."

Sera continued to cry into my shoulder while I rubbed her back. I felt like a jerk, because it was me who'd made her feel this way.

I wasn't afraid of Malevolent before. But after dealing with those wolves, I was scared out of my mind.

On Tuesday morning at dawn, I suppressed a yawn, knowing I had to be at my best today. Even before the school day began, the three of us were working on channeling the Unicorn's Lament, but I really wasn't feeling it. If Avalar wanted me to do this spell right, the least he could do was let me sleep.

"The Unicorn's Lament is a test of your powers. It is all the strength of your magic combined with your fellow princesses'. Done correctly, the spell will form a rainbow appearance," Avalar said.

"How do we cast it?" I asked. Avalar barely looked at me. He was still mad, obviously.

"The Unicorn's Lament is forged by combining the three values that are most important to the unicorns—friendship, beauty, and love," Avalar continued. "Each of you must embody and produce the truest form of this magic, and combine them together in order to stop Malevolent and break the dark magic that protects and controls her."

I raised an eyebrow at that. Did Avalar truly think that Malevolent didn't have a choice when it came to her use of dark magic? After all these years, did he really think he still stood a chance at getting back together with my mother?

"Stand in a triangle," Avalar said. He motioned for us to change, and we did. He positioned us at three points across from each other, then put a hay bale in the middle—a target that stood as Malevolent.

"Think of the truest form of your value to you, and use it to channel your magic," Avalar said. "Sera, you'll be given the value of beauty. Novah, friendship. And Thea, your value will be love."

I immediately focused. I tried to think of what love meant to me, and what I would consider the truest embodiment of it. My mind went blank, and I couldn't think of anything. I tried to think of Sera and of Ambrosia, and though I knew that I loved them and that they loved me, I didn't know why. I realized I didn't truly understand love, or beauty, or friendship.

On our first try, we merely managed to get multicolored sparks to fly from our horns. On the second, flashes of color popped out, but they were nothing like the beautiful rainbow I'd imagined. We struggled to combine our magic, and the rainbow that was supposed to result just ended up looking like a pastel-colored sludge all over the hay bale.

"This isn't working," Avalar said. "Let us try something else."

We switched roles, changing up the values each of us had to embody to see if we could perform the spell easier. A few times, the magic exploded on us and caused injuries. Avalar had to heal us with his horn.

"Again," Avalar demanded. "Get it right this time, girls."

I felt frustrated. Avalar didn't even know what he was doing. He'd never performed the spell himself. He could be teaching us totally wrong.

We broke for school, but as soon as class was over, we were back here practicing. By the end of the day, my knees were shaking with tiredness. Avalar noticed and said, "That's enough. We'll pick it up again tomorrow."

Sera and Novah sighed with relief. But I didn't feel relieved at all. We were so close to my birthday, and so close to Malevolent arriving, and we were totally unprepared.

≈

Avalar worked with us all week, from sunrise to sunset, and only took time off so we could go to school. We could almost, but not quite, pull off the Unicorn's Lament by Friday night. We'd gotten far enough that we could make the rainbows come out of our horns, but they wouldn't combine. None of us could perform our part of the spell properly on our own. Not even Sera.

Avalar was on the point of looking hopeless. "Stop," he said, after the hundredth time we'd tried and failed. "You'll exhaust your magic. It's too late now."

The three of us stood in the clearing, exhausted. Our heads hung so low our horns almost touched the ground.

"You have to be able to perform the Unicorn's Lament by tomorrow," Avalar said firmly, as if we didn't already know the obvious.

"What if we can't?" I objected.

"You must," Avalar insisted. "There's no other way."

He turned his back on us. "Get some sleep. You'll need to be ready when Malevolent comes."

The three of us looked at each other warily. I felt as prepared as a puppy going to a dragon fight.

"We should be together tonight," Sera voiced. "Let's have a sleepover, my house."

"We won't sleep if we're all together," I pointed out.

"We can try," Sera said, before she added, "I have a feeling sleep isn't going to happen for us, anyway. And I don't want to be alone."

The look on Novah's face, and probably mine too, said the same.

We headed to Sera's house. Lucindiana made us dinner—pasta primavera, which was my favorite—but we barely ate. None of us were really hungry. When Novah refused to have any ice cream or cake after, I knew something was seriously wrong with us.

Ambrosia and Esmeralda, Novah's nursemaid, had come over, too, to spend the night. It seemed the Etherian unicorns wanted to be as close together as possible.

Eventually, darkness approached. We left the house and headed into the woods, beyond the protective wards around the town and the stables, in order to fight Malevolent.

When we got into the woods, I saw a bunch of unicorns standing in a protective circle. All of them were stallions. Jas was among them, though he hadn't changed yet. All above us, dark clouds had gathered above the mountains. A storm was brewing.

"Jas!" Novah said. She threw her arms around him, and he hugged her tightly.

"Jas, what are you doing here?" I asked as we approached.

"I'm part of the Unicorn Guard," he said. "I'm a knight sworn to protect the monarchy, like Avalar. All of us will gladly lay down our lives to protect the three princesses."

"No one is sacrificing themselves tonight," I said. I looked at Sera, and she nodded.

"I'll make sure you guys are protected," Jas said. "Don't worry about me. I can last the night."

Jas leaned down and gave Novah a kiss on the lips. Novah stood completely still, and Jas brushed his hand through her hair as he pulled away.

"Princess," he said, and nodded his head.

Novah looked stunned, like she was floating on clouds. She gave a girlish sigh. "Okay, Jas kissed me. I'm ready to die now."

"No one's going to die," I told her sharply. "There's a bunch of us and one of Malevolent. We can still win, even if she has her minions."

"But we can't perform the Unicorn's Lament," Sera objected. She seemed depressed and hopeless. It wasn't like her, and I hated it.

"We can't yet, but maybe we should give it one more try," I suggested. "We might get it this time."

Sera's look of despair became one of determination. "Right. Let's do this."

By this time, it was around eleven o'clock. We tried again and again, but the spell wouldn't work. I could hardly make bubbles pop out of my horn at this rate. We all shifted back, looking desperate.

"This is useless!" Novah said. "We're never going to get it!"

"Don't give up!" I encouraged them, but even I was downtrodden. I didn't know if we could pull it off, either.

"I think I'm getting closer to figuring this out. We need to use the best parts of ourselves to beat her," Sera said firmly. "There's no other way."

"How are we supposed to do that?" Novah wailed. Sera didn't have an answer for her, and I didn't, either.

The dark clouds had only grown bigger and more foreboding. They covered the sky and blacked out any light from the moon or stars. Thunder rolled above my head, and I looked up at the exact time lightning rippled across the sky, making the clouds appear in fragmented cracks. The sound from the thunder was so loud, it made me jump. I could feel it vibrating in my bones.

Rain began pouring from the sky, and within seconds, that rain had turned to heavy hail. I put my arms up to shield myself from it. A storm was whipping up, the most powerful I'd ever seen.

"Girls!" Ambrosia called. "Get ready!"

The three of us huddled together. The knights shook their manes and steadied themselves against the hail that was pouring down.

I had a bad feeling I knew what was going on and where the storm had come from. I checked my watch. It was only an hour past midnight. My eyes met Sera's. She'd had the same thought. She wore the same horrified expression I did.

This couldn't be right. We had expected to have a little bit of time before she arrived. We were completely unprepared!

Yet Malevolent had wasted no time. She'd already broken out of her prison by the time the clock struck twelve.

And she was already here.

CHAPTER 10

*S*era, Novah, and I gathered together. We watched as hundreds of wolves streamed into the open area. The knights turned to face them, lights glowing from their horns. They began battling the wolves viciously. The hail increased, and we watched in horror as the wolves began to bring down some of the knights, in search of us.

"We have to find Malevolent," Sera said. She turned to look at us. "You girls with me?"

We weren't ready. But I knew we'd never be ready. The moment had come, and it was do or die.

"We're with you," I replied. "Now until the end."

"Let's go." Novah changed, and we did the same. Our maids—Ambrosia, Lucindiana, and Esmeralda—followed us.

Ambrosia was a beautiful unicorn. She was pure white, from her horn to her hooves. Lucindiana was lavender, and Esmeralda was orange. We raced through the battle, dodging the fighting that was going on all around us. The knights kept Malevolent's minions off us so we could search for the evil queen.

Thing was, I wasn't entirely sure I wanted to find her.

I saw a flash of silver in my peripheral vision. Avalar had arrived.

He galloped up beside me, and I noticed with horror part of his pelt was covered with blood—his blood.

"We need to get to the clearing!" Avalar shouted. *"Follow me!"*

Avalar turned and headed into the forest. Multiple minions went to follow us but knights blocked the way, chasing the wolves back with the light from their horns. Jas successfully burned three wolves that were hot on Novah's tail before he brought up his head to watch us race by.

"Jaspirion!" Avalar cried. *"We need you!"*

Jas left his post and took up the rear. The minute we entered the deeper forest, the world got even darker. The trees shielded us from the hail, but it was still difficult to know where we were going. We made light gleam from our horns so we could see.

Avalar slowed down to a walk. He was being cautious now. The rest of us allowed him to take the lead.

The sounds of battle and the howls of the wolves died out behind us.

But once we reached the clearing, there was someone already waiting for us.

Malevolent. She stood before us in her unicorn form, a devious gleam in her eye.

Her pelt was midnight blue, and she had a curled mane and tail that fell nearly to her hooves. A long cloak of starlight upon velvet hung from her shoulders, clasped in place by a gold brooch on her chest. Her horn was gone. She'd sold it to obtain dark magic, I remembered. In its place was a long, black icicle, curved like a knife and glinting like glass.

As we approached, Malevolent changed. She became a woman with long black hair, wearing a cobalt-blue velvet gown. A crown of black icicles glittered on top of her head, and her nails were long, painted, and sharp. Her skin was as pale as mine, and her eyes were brown and cold. She looked every part the evil queen from the darkest fairy tale I could imagine.

She was gorgeous. And the worst part of it was, I could see myself in her. We had the same facial features, same body structure. I'd taken little from Avalar. Besides my light hair, I was basically a younger copy of her.

As we approached, Malevolent opened her arms. "Aramanthe," she said. She gave a wide smile, revealing perfect teeth. "I've waited seventeen years to meet you again, my daughter."

Avalar changed back, and we all took it as a sign to do the same. Avalar stepped forward, planting himself in front of me.

"Surrender, Malestraude," he said. "You are outnumbered. Let us end this quietly."

My heart beat fast. Maybe we wouldn't have to fight. Maybe we could talk things out.

"Oh, I have no intention of talking. I did enough talking to myself, for nearly two decades while confined in a cage you helped put me in, Avalar," Malevolent said coolly. "You said you loved me. That clearly was a lie."

"I did love you. I don't love what you've become." Avalar stood his ground, but his expression seemed conflicted.

"I have no more business with you, Avalar," Malevolent said, and she waved her hand like she was disgusted. "My concern is with Aramanthe."

Malevolent extended a hand to me. "Come, my daughter. Take your rightful place by your mother's side. Together, we could rule the unicorns and Havenwood Falls. Our joined power would be unstoppable."

I shook my head and backed away to stand by Ambrosia. "I have a mother, and she isn't you."

Malevolent threw back her head and laughed. "The nursemaid? I have more power in my hooves than she has in her horn. Do you think she can protect you from me?"

"I will until my last breath," Ambrosia vowed. "Come close to her, and I'll spear you with my horn."

Malevolent chuckled, like this was a game and all of us were her pawns. "This is an embarrassing display. I've had enough of these jests."

Malevolent moved faster than any of us could think. In the blink of an eye, she transformed into a unicorn and sent a black bolt of magic shooting from her horn. It was directed at me, but since Avalar was standing in front of me, it hit him in the chest. He went down, making wheezing sounds with his chest.

"Avalar!" I cried. I rushed forward, putting my hands on his back. He was still struggling to breathe.

"It was a mistake to bring you here," Avalar gasped. His eyes seemed panicked and afraid.

"No." I shook my head. "No, it wasn't a mistake."

"Abandon the unicorns," Avalar breathed. "Run away, Thea. I just want to make sure you're safe."

"What a disgusting display of affection," Malevolent said. *"It's wholly boresome."*

She sent another black bolt at Avalar, but I pulled him out of the way and to the ground before it could hit him. Malevolent started firing, this time shooting bolts that looked like lightning from her horn. Sera and Novah dove out of the way, and our nursemaids sprang into action.

Ambrosia, Lucindiana, and Esmeralda charged at Malevolent from three different directions. Lucindiana sent a stream of vines from her horn, intending to wrap Malevolent within them, but Malevolent stepped aside and the vines wrapped around a tree instead. Malevolent aimed a lightning bolt at her, and it hit her target. Once Lucindiana was struck by the bolt, she froze in place. Marble began crawling across her pelt, and she was captured in an expression of fear and shock, her form completely made of stone.

All of us were frozen in shock as we looked at the statue of Lucindiana, frozen in place. Sera's screaming could be heard in the background.

While we were all distracted, Malevolent took her chance. She shot a beam at Esmeralda, and like Lucindiana, she became a statue.

"Esmeralda!" Novah screamed. She ran to her nursemaid and threw her arms around the statue, crying. Jas dragged Novah away from Esmeralda just before another one of Malevolent's bolts hit her.

Then my worst nightmare happened. Ambrosia reached

Malevolent, and the two mares rose up on their hind legs, batting their hooves at each other as they dueled. Malevolent's right hoof hit Ambrosia in the face, knocking her down. Ambrosia attempted to get back up, but Malevolent shocked her, and quick as a flash, the only mother I knew turned to stone.

"Ambrosia!" I screamed. I rushed to her and put my hands against her marble form, but she didn't move. She was captured in a prison of marble.

With the loss of Ambrosia, I went numb. If I didn't know what to do before, I was completely helpless now. I couldn't feel anything.

"You're going to pay for this!" Jas screamed. He lost his temper and transformed. Jas left Novah's side and galloped at Malevolent full speed with his horn down.

The moment he neared her, Malevolent spun around and kicked out with her back hooves. The blow caught Jas in the side of the head and sent him flying backward. He transformed mid-fall and slammed against a tree. He slumped against it, bleeding from a cut on the side of his head.

"Jas!" Novah went to his side, kneeling next to him and shaking him in an attempt to wake him up. But although he was still breathing, he was totally out of it.

She'd reduced us to four in a matter of seconds, and she hadn't even broken a sweat. It'd all happened so fast.

Malevolent changed back. The smile on her face was bigger than before. "Well, daughter, have you changed your mind?" she asked.

I backed away from her again. "I'll never join you!" I swore.

And I meant it. It didn't matter what she promised me. She'd turned Ambrosia to stone and hurt my dad. She could go to hell.

Malevolent's welcoming, generous smile instantly turned into a snarl of hatred. "Then perish!"

She shifted, and sent a lightning bolt at me. Everything from there happened in slow motion.

Avalar was no more than a few steps away. He was still recovering his breath, and noticed the spell Malevolent had cast in my direction.

"No! You won't take my daughter!" Avalar roared.

He changed into a unicorn and charged in front of Malevolent's blast. He reared up on his hind legs just as the spell hit him. Like Ambrosia, the spell spread until his form had become a statue and he was left frozen in place, an expression of rage and anguish on his face as his mane rippled behind him.

Avalar had sacrificed himself for me. The reality hit me like a landslide.

Sera, Novah, and I glanced at each other with panicked faces. We were alone. Malevolent had changed everyone to stone. Jas lay unconscious against a tree. We were on our own.

Malevolent went to attack me again, and I changed on instinct. I leapt out of the way just as she blasted a large hole in the tree behind me.

Sera and Novah changed, too. The three of us darted around the clearing and avoided Malevolent's blasts from her horn. We couldn't get close enough to hurt her with our horns or hooves. She sent spells so fast that it was difficult to think of any of our own.

One of the bolts was headed straight for me again. I managed to conjure up a magic shield just in time to stop the bolt from hitting me. Novah and Sera copied me, and Malevolent's spells bounced off and ricocheted everywhere. Defending ourselves was the best we could do in this situation.

This was impossible. We were overrun. We couldn't handle this. Malevolent was going to win.

Sera's words broke into my head. *"We need to use the best parts of ourselves to beat her."*

But the best parts of me weren't strong or brave or wise. The best parts of me were girly and playful and colorful. What use were those kinds of things in a fight to the death?

I figured we were dead anyway, and I might as well try something different. While she was distracted with chasing Novah and Sera, I used my horn to summon the biggest jet of bubbles I possibly could and sent them streaming at Malevolent full blast.

Malevolent wasn't expecting them. The blast of bubbles hit her in the face. Surprised by the onslaught, she stopped casting spells and backed away. She shook her head violently, her eyes full of bubble goo and temporarily blinded.

"*Girls, that's the key!*" I shouted to them. "*Think of something silly! Something happy!*"

Sera's and Novah's expressions were bewildered, but they did as I said. Sera sent fluffy blue hearts puffing out of her horn that surrounded Malevolent like a fog. When the hearts popped, they released a blue gas that filled Malevolent's mouth. She coughed and snorted, struggling to breathe.

Novah pointed at the ground, and green teddy bears popped up out of the dirt. Malevolent stepped on them, and they squeaked as she did, throwing her senses off further. She stumbled around and tripped, trying and failing to gain back her surroundings.

"*This is childish! Stop this behavior at once, and fight me!*" Malevolent demanded, still gasping for breath.

She sent more lightning bolts, but they were scattered and missed their target. She couldn't predict which spells we were going to cast next, as they were nonsensical. Their purpose was to throw her off her game, and it was working.

Novah sent a sticky pink substance out of her horn at Malevolent's hooves. It turned out to be gum. Malevolent tried to pull her hooves out of it, but even as she was able to free one hoof, another became stuck in the goo.

While Malevolent was held by the gum, Sera cast the magic trap. Malevolent stopped immediately within the circle, and struggled to break free.

She could've if she gathered her bearings. But I kept Malevolent disoriented with the bubbles while Sera grew the power of the magic trap and Novah kept tossing teddy bears that hit her in the face. Novah was laughing as she did so. Malevolent looked furious.

"*When I break this spell, the three of you are going to be begging for mercy,*" Malevolent snarled. Her mouth and eyes were the only part of her that she could move now. The magic trap had her bound.

"*Girls! The Unicorn's Lament!*" I cried. "*Do it now!*"

The three of us galloped to our places to form the triangle. We only had a few moments before Malevolent would be able to break out of the magic trap. We had to move quickly.

There was no doubt we could do it. We had to. I closed my eyes and thought about how Avalar had sacrificed himself for me, and all that he had done to keep me safe, even if he couldn't be there while I was growing up—even if he wanted to. I understood what love was in that moment and had never felt more powerful in all my life.

"For love!" I cried.

"For beauty!" Sera added.

"For friendship!" the three of us said at once. We sent colors shooting from the tips of our horns, and in the air, the three spells combined to make a rainbow that vibrated with intensity and power. As the rainbow claimed her, Malevolent began to scream in fury. Her form waved and dipped within the colors as she tried to escape and failed.

"You might be powerful, but you're no match for the Equestriad!" I yelled triumphantly. *"You're finished!"*

Malevolent gave one last scream of rage before the rainbow overtook her, and she exploded into an array of colorful sparkles. They coated the area and gleamed throughout the clearing, trailing through the air to the ground like falling stars.

The three of us looked at each other in amazement. We had done it. Malevolent was defeated.

Once Malevolent was gone, the unicorns that had become statues turned back to normal. Ambrosia, Lucindiana, Esmeralda, and Avalar broke free from the marble, emerging from the stone in their human forms.

"Ambrosia!" I screamed. I threw myself into her arms and hugged her tightly. Beside me, Sera and Novah did the same with their nursemaids.

"Thea, I'm so proud of you." Ambrosia put her face in my hair, and I felt her tears soaking into my head. "You're truly the princess everyone knew you would be."

"Thanks, Mom." I pulled away from her and wiped the tears from her eyes.

I turned. Avalar had come out of his statue, and he was staring at me.

"Well done, Thea," he said gruffly. "I always knew you had it in you."

I looked at him. Then I ran forward and embraced him as tightly as I could, trying to thank him for what he had done. There weren't any words I could say that would indicate how much gratitude I felt in that moment.

Avalar stiffened with the touch, like he didn't know how to react, before he relaxed and wrapped his arms around me.

"You don't know how long I've waited to hold you in my arms," he said. "Since the moment I gave you away."

"You don't know how long I've waited to have a dad," I whispered back.

Avalar pulled away and tweaked my chin. "What do you say we go for a gallop later?" he asked. "Just some father-daughter time."

"That sounds amazing." Images of me and Avalar galloping through the forest together, as silver and pink unicorns, burst into my mind. It was more than I had ever hoped for or dreamed of growing up.

There was a groan behind us. Jas was waking up. Novah was at his side, helping him sit up and looking concerned.

Jas blinked his eyes wearily, looking around the scene of crushed marble, gum, and teddy bears. He shook his head once or twice, then slurred, "Hey. Who am I?"

We had lost a few knights in the fight, but the unicorns had emerged victorious. Avalar had organized a party at Creekwood Country Club that night, to celebrate my birthday and the fact that Malevolent was finally defeated. The unicorns could live on in peace.

I wore a big dress, the pinkest and the prettiest I owned, along with high heels and a big, glittering tiara. Sera and Novah wore gowns in their respective colors, tiaras on their heads, too.

Everywhere we went, unicorns bowed to us and said, "Princesses." It was surreal.

The food at the country club was so good. Avalar had rented out a large empty space with a dance floor, and a DJ played all of the Equestriad's favorite songs. Sera, Novah, and I danced all night with the rest of the unicorns, who, I learned, did love something more than sugar—and that was getting down with their bad selves.

I was surprised Avalar had thrown the party together so quickly, until I learned that he'd been planning it all month as a surprise for me. He assumed that we could defeat Malevolent. He hadn't even had a doubt, as he'd already paid for the food and the deposit for the ballroom.

He'd believed in me all along. He just wanted to push me to succeed.

While Sera, Novah, and I were dancing, a familiar face appeared. Jas was there, wearing a suit with his head bandaged in thick white wrappings.

"Hey, girls," he said. "Happy birthday, Thea."

"Jas! So nice of you to come," Sera said politely.

"Are you sure you should be here?" Novah asked, looking worriedly at the wrappings around his head.

"It's just a small concussion," Jas said. "I'll be fine. The doctors wanted me to rest, but I never miss a party."

Jas took Novah in his arms and spun her around a few times. Novah giggled, lighting up as he twirled her around.

"It's so sweet that you guys get to be princesses," Jas said offhandedly. "At least for a day."

The three of us looked at each other with wary expressions. "Yes," I said. "Of course."

"I'm starving, by the way," Jas said. "I'm gonna grab a plate. Coming, Novah?"

She shook her head. "I'll be there in a minute."

"All right. Don't keep me waiting." He gave her a wink, then whirled around on his heel and went to the buffet line.

Novah seemed crushed. Sera put her hand on Novah's shoulder.

"He'll come back to you, Novah," Sera said gently. "Give him time."

Novah gave a watery smile. "I hope so."

Jas had amnesia from Malevolent's strike to his head. He'd forgotten that he was a unicorn, about Malevolent . . . everything. He thought that this was just a normal birthday party.

Avalar said it was best to let Jas remember everything on his own, and allow him to think he was a regular human for a while. There was no telling how he'd react if we told him the truth about everything, or if he'd believe us.

He'd also forgotten he'd kissed Novah. Which was devastating to her.

"It's okay. I've got my girls," Novah said, and she threw her arms over Sera's shoulder and mine. "The Equestriad's all we need, as long as we're together." Then she frowned. "So long as you two lovers don't treat me like a third wheel."

"We would never do that to you," Sera said.

"Yeah," I agreed. "Besides, we're going to make great aunts, once Jas's memory comes back and you two start making all kinds of cute unicorn babies."

"Shut up!" Novah laughed, and slapped me on the arm.

A slow song came on. Novah left the floor, presumably to look for Jas. I reached out and grabbed Sera, taking her into my arms. Couples flooded onto the dance floor.

We swayed slowly to the music, all the other unicorn couples twirling around us. Avalar looked on proudly from the sidelines, Ambrosia next to him.

"Do you believe in fairy tales?" Sera asked sweetly. She straightened the crown on my head, and spun me around before bringing me close once again.

"Yes," I replied. "I'm living in one."

As the song went on, Sera laid her head on my chest. Just before it ended, I whispered in her ear, "Sera?"

"Hm?" She lifted her head and looked at me.

I wasn't afraid to ask now. "Do you want to be my girlfriend?"

Sera smiled at me. She leaned over and gave me a deep kiss, taking my hands in hers. "Thea, I think that would be the most magical thing of all."

We hope you enjoyed this story in the Havenwood Falls High series of novellas featuring a variety of supernatural creatures. The series is a collaborative effort by multiple authors. If you loved this story, you might also enjoy these:

Somewhere Within by Amy Hale
Reclamation by AnnaLisa Grant
Avenoir by Daniele Lanzarotta

Stay up to date at www.HavenwoodFalls.com

ABOUT THE AUTHOR

Megan Linski is a *USA Today* bestselling author and a disabled writer from Michigan. She writes books for teens and young adults in the fantasy and romance genres. She enjoys ice skating, horse riding, and traveling the world. In her spare time, she advocates for mental health awareness and suicide prevention, and also battles Common Variable Immune Deficiency Disorder, a rare primary immune condition.

You can find her at www.meganlinski.com.

ACKNOWLEDGMENTS

Thank you to all the Havenwood Falls authors who allowed me to use your characters in my story— Kristie Cook for Addie, Liz Ferry for Celeste and Jonathan, E.J. Fechenda for Willow and Dalton, and Amy Hale for Miranda. It was quite the magical experience!

HAVENWOOD FALLS HIGH

Paper Bird

AMY RICHIE

~ A Havenwood Falls Young Adult Novella ~

Paper Bird (A Havenwood Falls High Novella) by Amy Richie

One little stolen shirt and my uncle sends me to live with my dad in some weird little town in Colorado.

Ava Tate has never had what anyone would call a fairytale life. A dead mother, an absent father, and an uncle who doesn't want her. One more year of high school and she'll be able to live on her own. But after another run-in with the cops, her uncle sends her away to live with a father she's never even met before in a town she's never heard of.

How will she survive an entire year stuck in the mountains?

Ava isn't counting on meeting Toby, though. Suddenly, all the rules seem to be changing, and if she doesn't keep up, her very existence will be wiped away. After Toby tells her what she really is, Ava finds out that some don't believe her kind should exist at all. Ava must come to terms with a truth that was buried with her mother, or this paper bird will be destroyed.

PAPER BIRD

BY AMY RICHIE

The air was crisp with an October chill. Up ahead, he could make out the bar where Elias had asked to meet him. He still wasn't sure what this meeting was all about, but when his old friend had called, Ralph couldn't resist his desire to meet him again after so many years apart.

Elias had fallen off the grid completely, almost like he was gone from Earth, but Ralph knew better than that. Elias was one of the few angels left here that he could trust.

Inside the bar, an old country song blared from the jukebox. In one corner, a couple was so twisted up in each other, it was hard to tell where one stopped and the other began. His heart clenched a little for his Beth. If she were here, they would be in a similar position.

He quickly shook his head to dispel such thoughts. He was here to meet Elias, and then he would go home and . . . He grinned as his thoughts ran away from him again.

"Ralph," a familiar voice boomed out. A dark-haired man waved from a stool at the bar; Ralph hurried to join him.

"Elias." He smiled wide. "It's been a long time, my friend."

"Indeed it has." Elias beamed back at him. "Sit. I'll buy you a drink."

Ralph sipped on his drink while he listened to Elias talk about the town he had come from.

"Sounds pretty . . . ideal," he commented when Elias took a breath. Being an angel himself, Ralph knew what a town that offered that kind of protection must mean to Elias.

"It is," he agreed, "but that isn't why I asked you to meet me."

"Then?"

"I've been hearing some . . . rumors about you."

Ralph stiffened slightly. "What kind of rumors?"

"Word is that you've become attached to a human."

His eyes narrowed as he took a forced drink. "I don't see how that is any of your concern."

Elias's hand tightened around his drink. "I'm only looking out for you, friend. There are some who won't take kindly to your . . . transgressions."

"What exactly are you trying to say?"

"I'm telling you to end this before it's too late."

Ralph stood up from his stool. "Are you threatening me?"

"Not at all," he said calmly. "Just trying to help."

"Did Daniel send you to talk to me?" He ran a hand over his face. He was a fool to think he could trust Elias. "What I do isn't any of your business, and you can tell Daniel that too."

"I'm not here for him."

"Whatever."

"If you run into trouble, come to this town of safe haven. They might be able to help you there."

"I don't need anyone's help."

Ralph was fuming as he slid off his stool and stormed out of the bar. So Elias was doing favors for Daniel now? Who did they think they were to tell him what to do? He didn't take orders from anyone. His feet slapped against the pavement as he made his way toward the only person who offered him any comfort these days.

Her.

∾

PRESENT DAY - AVA

I sucked in a deep breath and held it in my aching chest. Pushing my senses out, I could just make out the argument going on in front of me —on the big porch attached to an equally large farm house.

"Did you get my letter?" Uncle Ted asked the man who hadn't stopped scowling since we pulled up.

"Mail's slow here," he grunted in reply.

"If I had your phone number . . ."

"No phone."

"Ava is in the car." He jerked his thumb back to me.

From my distance I couldn't be sure, but I thought I saw the man's eyes bug out. "Why?"

"If you would have read my letter . . ." He scowled, letting his words trail off in a grumble.

"Why is she here?"

"There's been more trouble."

"What kind of trouble?"

"The girl can't stay out of jail."

I sank lower into the seat. There was no reason for me to hear this part, no matter how exceptional my hearing was. Uncle Ted and his lovely wife Jane didn't want someone like me around their perfect children. I was a bad influence.

Or so I had been told.

"Hey." Uncle Ted was suddenly back at the car, yanking open my door. "You can come out now."

"I thought you said we were coming to see my dad."

"What?" Distracted, he pressed on the trunk button that was hidden in the glove compartment. "We are," he grunted, still close to my face. "That's him up there."

I peered through the glass at the man glowering at us. He couldn't have been more than a few years older than me. Why was Uncle Ted lying?

"Come on out now," he ordered curtly, moving around to the back of the car to take out my suitcases.

Reluctantly, I pushed the door open farther and stepped out onto the unfamiliar grass. So this was where they were banishing me to? For one stolen shirt?

I really hated being a bad influence.

Uncle Ted had already dug all my things from the trunk and had most of it tucked in his arms and in his hands by the time I reached him—clearly he was in a hurry and I wasn't moving fast enough.

"I got these," he panted when I offered to help. I had little choice but to follow him back up to the house.

"Ralph." Uncle Ted reached out to the man who was obviously not old enough to be my father. "This is Ava."

Ralph's mouth fell open and stayed that way.

Now that I was closer, it was clear that something was different about Ralph, something I couldn't put my finger on. Even if Uncle Ted and Jane wanted to get rid of me, it wasn't right to just dump me off with a stranger in a town I had never heard of. We had a hard time finding the place; that should have been a sign.

"Who are you really?" I asked Ralph.

"He's your father," Uncle Ted sputtered. "I know this is—"

"He's not my dad," I cut him off. "He's too young."

"Well . . ." Uncle Ted rubbed his hand across his top lip.

"How did you find me?" Ralph asked, suddenly finding his voice again. "You shouldn't be here."

"We did get lost," Uncle Ted admitted, still not acting like himself. It must have been the stress of abandoning me when he promised his sister that he would take care of her only daughter. "There was a man —Brad, I think he said his name was—he pointed us in the right direction."

"We followed a bus," I piped in, taking pity on Uncle Ted and his stutters. I had never seen him so flustered.

Ralph's eyes strayed to me, as if he'd just remembered I was standing there. "Brad." He snorted. "Figures."

"So"—Uncle Ted cleared his throat—"anyways . . ."

"She can't stay here," Ralph suddenly snapped. "I don't want her."

Uncle Ted had the decency to shoot me a look of pity. "She . . . needs somewhere to go."

"She can go back with you."

"We don't . . ." He cleared his throat again. "She can't stay with us."

I was glad he hadn't said out loud that he didn't want me either. I mean, it was pretty obvious, but at least he didn't say it out loud.

"I'm . . ." Uncle Ted took a deep breath. "I'm sorry how this all worked out. If your mom . . ."

Was he really going to say he wouldn't dump me off here if she didn't die? If I hadn't killed her?

"Whatever." I shrugged. "Hope you and Jane . . . you know . . . do your thing." Despite how it was ending, I had lived with Uncle Ted for the last seventeen years. If nothing else, he was comfortable, and until he married Jane, he was even kind of nice.

"Yeah."

There were no tears or hugs or heartfelt goodbyes. He gave one last shrug, then slouched off the porch and practically ran back to his waiting car. If he got his way, I would never see Uncle Ted again. Feeling sad would have been appropriate, I realized. Too bad I couldn't bring myself to it.

"Hey," Ralph screamed, running off the porch after him. "I said you can't leave her here."

Uncle Ted was already pulling out of the driveway, though— without me. He didn't turn around.

"Ted!" Ralph stood alone in his front yard, screaming after the retreating car. All that was missing were the chickens and the beer-stained T-shirt, and this would be an episode on a reality TV show. "Come back here!"

Could today get any worse?

"He left," Ralph panted, stopping in front of me. "He just left."

"I noticed."

"You can't stay here."

My eyes slid closed and then opened again slowly. "I'll be eighteen soon."

"In seven months," he thundered.

It came as a bit of a shock that he knew my birthday. "Did you even know my dad?"

"Umm." He pinched the bridge of his nose. "I guess so."

"And my mom?"

At this, his hands dropped back down to his sides. "What did you do to get kicked out?"

"Stole a shirt." I shrugged, glancing down at the offending top. It wasn't even worth all the trouble I had gotten into, ten bucks at the most. Why didn't I just pay for it? "Is there a room in there I can use?"

His lips pursed tightly, but when he spoke again, his voice was soft. "Just until we get this figured out. A night . . . maybe two."

Purchase *Paper Bird* where books are sold.

www.ingramcontent.com/pod-product-compliance
Lightning Source LLC
Chambersburg PA
CBHW052015170626
46808CB00007B/2946